THE DUKE IS BACK

THE FOOTMEN'S CLUB SERIES

VALERIE BOWMAN

JUNE THIRD ENTERPRISES, LLC

The Duke is Back, copyright © 2022 by June Third Enterprises, LLC.

Print edition ISBN: 978-1-7368417-5-4

Digital edition ISBN: 978-1-7368417-4-7

Book Cover Design © Lyndsey Llewellen at Llewellen Designs.

For my darling boo boo, Sophie Hand.
An evil stepmother book just for you.

A wedding is in her future

Miss Sophie Payton might be engaged, but she's *not* in love. The only man who ever captured her heart was Phillip Grayson—a soldier who was slain a year ago. But when her stepmother decrees that Sophie will marry Phillip's cousin, the new Duke of Harlowe, Sophie's in no position to refuse.

A funeral is in his past

The *ton* thinks Phillip Grayson died a hero on the battlefields of Europe, but he's very much alive. While he spent the last year recuperating from his grave injuries in secret at his friend's estate, his brother was murdered, his cousin took over the title of duke, and the woman he loved—the one he dreamed of every night—apparently moved on without him.

But the duke is back

Phillip has returned to London intent on reclaiming his brother's title and making the people who killed him pay. He doesn't understand how Sophie could have betrayed him; she can't forgive him for letting her believe he was dead. And yet neither can deny that the attraction between them burns hotter than ever. Nothing is as it seems, but perhaps the truth can save them…if it doesn't kill them first.

AUTHOR'S NOTE

The Duke is Back is the sixth book in The Footmen's Club series. If you've read the other books, you know that the timeline hasn't been linear. After the first three books, I wrote the others in the order I wanted to tell the stories. So…to shed some light on the timeline, I hope the following helps. WARNING: SPOILERS! If you haven't read the other books yet, you may want to just skip to chapter one.

October 1813
Clayton and Theodora had their love affair (broken leg and all) and Phillip was at Clayton's house recuperating. Phillip had been with Clayton since summer of 1813.
This story is told in book 4, *Save a Horse, Ride a Viscount.*

Spring of 1814
This book, book 6, *The Duke is Back,* takes place in the spring after Clayton and Theodora marry. It's before the house party where the other heroes pretend to be servants. During this time, the Duke of Worthington was recuperating at home from being shot in France and staying away from

Julianna. Bell has yet to meet Marianne, and Kendall hasn't yet met Frances. The Bidassoa traitor isn't on Bell's radar yet. And the rightful Duke of Harlowe is about to return to London for the Season.

Late Summer of 1814 – Autumn of 1815

The infamous house party with Kendall, Bell, and Worth pretending to be servants. These stories are told in books 1-3, *The Footman and I* (Kendall), *Duke Looks Like a Groomsman* (Worth) and *The Valet Who Loved Me* (Bell).

Spring of 1815

The three couples from books 1-3 marry and Annabelle (Bell's sister) and David (Marianne's brother) get together. This story is told in book 5, *Earl Lessons*.

CHAPTER ONE

London, May 1814

Phillip Grayson was on his way to a ball, and not just any ball, a ball where all the attendees believed he was dead. He sat inside a luxurious carriage belonging to his friend, Viscount Clayton, as the conveyance pulled to a stop in front of the Cranberrys' town house. The Season had begun barely a fortnight ago, but this was the first event Phillip had attended. Indeed, it would be the only social event he'd been to in well over three years. He glanced out the window at the groups of finely dressed partygoers making their way toward the Cranberrys' front door.

Phillip swallowed hard. That was a lot of people. There would be even more in the ballroom. He hadn't been in a crowd in nearly a year. And the last one hadn't been filled with beautifully dressed partygoers laughing and sipping champagne. Far from it. It had been on a battlefield in Spain. And he had lain dying on the packed earth, the screams of his countrymen ringing in his ears, the smell of gunpowder burning his nose while his blood soaked into the soil, and the world around him went black.

Phillip clenched his jaw. Such thoughts wouldn't help him tonight. He must focus. He'd spent *months* preparing for this moment. And he was ready. He was. He needed all his wits about him. There was no telling how everyone would react to the proof that the rightful Duke of Harlowe was very much alive and (seemingly) well.

"Ready?" Clayton's wife, Thea, asked, giving him an encouraging smile from the opposite seat. Thea was as kind as she was beautiful, with her dark hair and inquisitive gray eyes.

Phillip nodded. "I'm thankful to have you two at my side tonight." While Phillip and Clayton had been friends since childhood, Phillip and Thea had become close while he'd recovered from his injuries over the last year. She'd reintroduced him to his horse, Alabaster, who Clayton had purchased at auction after the Arabian was returned to London from the Continent…from the war.

"Don't worry," Clayton said. "Follow me."

A footman opened the door to the coach and the viscount alighted first, turning to help his lady. Phillip soon followed, smoothing a hand down his white shirt front and black waistcoat. It had been an age since he'd been dressed in such fine evening attire. His clothing had been much more casual at Clayton Manor, and before that, as a captain in the army, he'd worn a uniform for years.

"I never expected to be back here," he said as he took a deep breath and stared up at the town house as if it were a ghost.

"The Cranberrys' house?" Thea asked, her brow slightly furrowed.

"London," Phillip clarified. He expelled his breath and gestured to Clayton to lead the way. "Shall we?"

Clayton started toward the front door while a hundred possible scenarios played through Phillip's mind. How would everyone react to his arrival? He'd gone over each scenario during the last months to prepare himself, but nerves were still getting the best of him tonight. He must tamp them down. They had no place in his performance this evening. He'd spent the better part of the last year at Clayton's estate in Devon, hidden away from London and Society, recuperating both physically and mentally from the shots that had knocked him off Alabaster in battle and nearly taken his life. He'd been planning tonight for months. It was time to take his rightful place in Society.

His wounds had healed quickly, but the worst pain had come a couple of months afterward, when he was strong enough for Clayton to inform him that his older brother, Malcolm, was dead. Not only that, but Clayton's good friend the Marquess of Bellingham—a spy for the Home Office— had reason to believe that Malcolm had been murdered.

Until today, the only people who knew Phillip was alive were Clayton, Thea, Bellingham—known as Bell to his friends—and Bell's superior officer at the Home Office, General Grimaldi. Grimaldi had finally allowed Phillip to quietly inform his mother just this afternoon. The poor woman had believed all this time that both her sons—her only children—were dead.

Without telling her why, Clayton had asked Phillip's mother to visit him at his town house earlier today. The look on her face when Phillip had walked through the doors of Clayton's drawing room had nearly made Phillip weep. She'd collapsed against the settee while Phillip had rushed over to hug her. "I'm sorry, Mother. I couldn't tell you till now."

Thankfully, Mother hadn't asked many questions and had agreed to keep the news of Phillip's return a secret until he revealed himself to Society tonight. She had reacted with pure joy this afternoon, hugging him and smoothing his hair as if he were still a boy and not a man nearly thirty years of age. The memory made Phillip smile.

There was only one other person whose reaction he cared about as much. And she was most likely standing in the Cranberrys' ballroom right now. The thought sent both a frisson of awareness and a tingle of apprehension through him.

Phillip took another deep breath. Why, again, had Grimaldi and Bell thought this was the way to do it? Oh, yes. The element of surprise. They had several operatives stationed about the ballroom tonight, watching for reactions from certain guests. Guests who might have had reason to want Malcolm dead.

Phillip, Clayton, and Thea made their way up the steps to the town house as carriages continued to drop off more guests behind them. Thankfully, no one appeared to have noticed Phillip yet. He was wearing a hat and coat and was shrouded in shadows. But it would only be a matter of moments before he entered the house, then the ballroom. He would doff his outerwear and the butler would call out his name. And then...

All hell would likely break loose.

Phillip swallowed and kept his gaze trained on Clayton's back. There was no better man than his friend. Clayton and Thea would ensure that Phillip made it through this night in one piece.

At the front door, an underbutler allowed them in, barely giving Phillip a second glance. He breathed a sigh of relief. After doffing their cloaks, gloves, and hats, the three of them continued up the grand staircase to the ballroom. They paused in front of the carved double doors to the enormous room.

"Ready?" Clayton said this time, giving Phillip an encouraging grin.

Phillip lifted his chin and straightened his shoulders. "As I expect to be."

Thea gave him a quick smile and a reassuring squeeze on his elbow. "You'll be magnificent," she said. "And we'll be with you every step."

Clayton pushed open the double doors. The butler stood just inside the entrance. As Clayton leaned over and whispered in the butler's ear, Phillip kept his gaze trained directly in front of him at the blur of light and sound that made up the crowded ballroom. It was loud and bright and filled with people. His throat began to close. But he did what Forrester —the man who had helped him recover—had told him to do. He concentrated on one moment, one breath at a time. *Breathe in. Breathe out. Three. Two. One.*

"Lord and Lady Clayton, and...*the Duke of Harlowe*," the butler intoned. The man's voice was clear and strong, but there had definitely been both a pause and an emphasis on his title. Phillip's jaw clenched. *Breathe in. Breathe out.*

A pin hitting the polished parquet floor would have made a racket. The chattering ceased. The music stopped. All eyes in the ballroom turned to stare at the three of them.

Lady Cranberry, in dark-red skirts that aptly matched her name, came rushing toward them from her spot in the receiving line.

"Higgins, you must be mistaken," she said, addressing her remarks to the butler. "This cannot be—" She turned to look at their trio and her face immediately turned ashen white. "Y...Your Grace," she breathed, putting a ring-laden hand to her throat.

Phillip smiled at the woman and tipped his head toward her. He hadn't seen her in quite some time, but she looked nearly the same as she had the last time he'd been at a London ball. "Lady Cranberry," he intoned.

A strange noise that sounded like a cross between a hysterical laugh and a deep sob issued from the lady's mouth before she managed to say, "I'd no idea you'd…" She cleared her throat and shook her head slightly. "Welcome, *Your Grace*. Welcome. Welcome." She dipped into a deep curtsy.

The poor, flustered woman turned to the occupants of the ballroom and called out as if confirming that she'd verified with her own eyes, "The Duke of Harlowe, *Phillip Grayson*, is here. Please, do carry on."

Everyone spoke at once, and they were all talking about him, staring at him.

Breathe in. Breathe out.

Phillip gave Clayton and Thea a solid nod. He knew his friends were worried about him. But Phillip had expected this. He was prepared. He was done hiding. He *would* avenge his brother's murder.

Their small group had barely taken more than a few steps into the ballroom when a dark-haired young woman in a sapphire evening gown broke away from a cluster in the middle of the ballroom and came toward them. Phillip watched her come. Her walk was familiar. Her curly dark-brown hair and even darker eyes—also familiar—came into focus as she neared. She moved inexorably toward him until she was standing directly in front of him. This was it. The moment he'd both anticipated and feared for nearly a year.

She searched his face. Tears welled in her eyes, but there was something else. A hint of unmistakable anger flashed there, too. Her lovely features had hardened into a mask of stone. "Phillip?" she breathed. The name sounded like an accusation.

He felt her voice like a stab to the chest. He hadn't heard it in…three years. All this time, he'd only had her letters. The letters he'd lost during the war. All save the one that had been next to his heart when he'd been shot off Alabaster's back and left for dead.

She was older now, a bit too thin. Sadness was etched in the tiny lines at the corners of her eyes. But it still physically hurt to look at her. She was so beautiful.

He'd dreamed of this moment many times over the last three years, but it had never been like this. And he regretted it had to be this way now. He regretted it very much.

SOPHIE TOOK A DEEP, shaky breath. Phillip, the man she'd loved for so long, the man she'd believed to be *dead* for nearly the past *year*, was standing in front of her very much alive.

She swallowed hard, struggling to keep the tears that burned the backs of her eyes from falling.

"It's really you," she said, close enough to him now to see the small lines in his face, the familiar emerald color of his eyes, the tiny scar just below his lip. And she could smell him, too. The same familiar scent of soap and sandalwood that threatened to send her memory soaring back to an entirely different time and place. A time and place that now seemed like a century ago.

Just then, a thunderous crash sounded behind them. Sophie jumped and whirled to see a footman with a full silver tray of champagne flutes shattered at his feet. The ungodly racket had stopped time for a moment. When she turned back again to Phillip, his eyes were glossy, and he was staring straight ahead as if completely sightless.

"Phillip?" She uttered his name again with all the pain and anger that was colliding in her heart. She wanted to reach for him. She wanted to slap him.

He didn't even glance at her. Sweat beaded on his brow as

he continued to stare at the far end of the ballroom as if in a trance. The pretty young woman beside him—Lady Clayton, was it?—reached out and laid a hand on his arm. "It's all right, Phillip."

Sophie clenched her jaw. *All right?* Was Lady Clayton somehow trying to comfort Phillip given Sophie's presence?

She searched his face again. He still wouldn't look at her. An icy dread seeped into her middle. So this was how it would be? Phillip was intent upon ignoring her? So be it. He'd left her. He'd allowed her to believe he was dead all these months. And now he was looking right through her, with another woman's hand on his arm.

Sophie's own hand itched to slap him across his handsome face. Anything to garner some reaction from him besides his apathy. But no. She would not stoop to theatrics and common violence. She was better than that. She'd already survived losing him once. She could do it again.

Summoning all the strength she had, Sophie sucked in her breath, turned immediately on her heels, lifted her chin, and walked away. If Phillip Grayson intended to ignore her, intended to pretend as if they had meant nothing to each other...by God, she would do the same.

CHAPTER TWO

Sophie marched away. But *not* back to her stepmother and the others she'd been standing with when the butler had called out the Duke of Harlowe's name. She had glanced over, expecting to see Hugh, wondering why he would arrive with people named Lord and Lady Clayton.

Sophie strode straight out of the ballroom, down the corridor and into the ladies' retiring room, which was thankfully empty. Still shaking, she pressed a hand to her middle, quite certain she might cast up her accounts.

Nothing could have prepared her for the pure shock that had hit her like a kick to the middle when she'd looked over to see not Hugh, but *Phillip* standing there. Phillip with his unmistakable height, his shining blond hair, and his bright green eyes. Phillip, the man she'd been in love with for years and had believed to be *dead* for the past eleven months. When she'd first seen him tonight, Sophie had been torn between wanting to slap him and wanting to hug him until her arms gave out. Neither of which were proper.

Where in the world had he been all this time? And why, why, hadn't he sent word that he was alive and well? There had been a part of her—some hopeful, foolish part—that had wanted to believe the moment he saw her, he'd tug her into his arms and declare himself.

Instead, he'd done nearly the opposite. He'd looked past her as if she wasn't even there. Hadn't even responded when she'd said his name. Hadn't said one word to her, in fact. She'd have thought he was an imposter, but for the fact that she knew with every fiber of her soul that he wasn't. She knew his face so well. There was no doubt. That had definitely been Phillip Grayson standing there. But apparently, he was no longer the man she'd known for three years.

Sophie lifted her gaze and stared at herself in the looking glass. At least she hadn't cried. She had that small bit of comfort. God knew tears had been wavering in her eyes the entire time. She'd no idea how her legs had had the strength to remain upright. Now she felt as if she might melt to the floor, a puddle on the fine rug. She blew out a deep breath. The same thoughts circled in her head once again. What in the world was Phillip doing here? And where had he been all this time? And why in the name of all that was holy had he let her believe he was dead?

The questions chased each other around and around in Sophie's mind. Now that she thought on it, she probably should have asked him any of those questions. But it was too late. And given his behavior, she suspected he wouldn't have answered either. She'd been left to stand in front of him like a fool, waiting for some sort of acknowledgement that never came.

She should have slapped him. It was the least he deserved after putting her through the last year of hell. But striking him would have been improper. Imprudent. Wrong.

She paced away from the mirror, biting the tip of her finger. Oh, dear. *Think*. For the first time since hearing his name come out of Lady Cranberry's mouth, a rush of awful realizations sped through Sophie's mind. She may not have slapped Phillip, but how had it looked to the occupants of the ballroom? The moment he walked in the door, she rushed up to him and received the cut direct. Her engagement to Hugh Grayson, Phillip's first cousin, who had claimed the title, had just been announced in the papers this very morning. The entire *ton* would be gossiping about whether she would still go through with the wedding now that Phillip, the *rightful* duke, was apparently back.

She didn't *care* about her engagement, of course. She hadn't cared about anything since she'd got the news all those awful months ago that Phillip had been killed on the Continent. She'd spent the year quietly grieving for the man she loved without being able to tell a soul, while her stepmother, Valentina, had insisted she find a husband. And not just any husband. "You'll be a duchess one day, Sophia," Valentina always said. The woman had had a triumphant smile on her face a fortnight ago when she'd announced that Papa and Hugh had signed the betrothal agreement. Of course, Sophie had not understood they intended to announce the betrothal so soon. They hadn't even consulted her. Its appearance in this morning's paper had been a complete surprise. She couldn't help but quirk her lips in a small smile. It looked as if her *dear* stepmother would no longer get her wish. She seriously doubted Valentina would want her to marry Hugh now that it was obvious the man would go back to being untitled.

Come to think of it...where *was* Hugh? He'd been planning to come tonight, or so he'd said the last time they spoke. Had he known his cousin was coming back from the dead to claim the title that had been his for the last nine months? If he *had* known, surely he would have told her. Or at least he would have told Valentina. Wouldn't he?

Sophie forced herself to take another deep breath. The

last thing she wanted to do was go back out there and face the partygoers. Any of them. Not Hugh, *if* he'd arrived. Not Valentina. Not the ladies of the *ton* who had just finished offering their best wishes, but who would now stare at her with pity in their eyes. And certainly not Phillip. Least of all Phillip.

She pushed herself off the wall and straightened her shoulders. Only a coward would remain hiding in this room for the rest of the night. And she was no coward. She had to return to the ballroom or the gossip would be unmanageable. She pinched her cheeks, causing a hint of pink to spring back into them from the ghastly white they had been.

She turned toward the door of the retiring room just as it swung open, and her stepmother came sweeping in. Valentina's blood-red gown barely covered her ample breasts. Her black hair was piled high atop her head and held in place by a diamond tiara that Papa could ill afford. Valentina's silver-green eyes narrowed to slits. "There you are, Sophia. Thank heavens I found you." Everything Valentina said sounded like either a purr or a hiss.

Sophie clenched her jaw. "I was just coming back." She'd never had a pleasant encounter with her stepmother, and she had every reason to believe those sorts of interactions wouldn't begin now. No doubt the woman wanted to know why she'd approached Phillip Grayson.

Never one to pass a looking glass without making full use of it, Valentina stared at herself in the *cheval* and pursed her lips. She ran a tapered fingertip along one black eyebrow and turned her head from side to side, no doubt admiring her own beauty. And there wasn't any doubt. Valentina *was* beautiful. At five and twenty, she was only five years older than Sophie herself. Papa, who'd been a widower since Sophie was eight years old—had had his head turned by the woman's looks five years ago. Her *disposition* certainly wasn't anything to covet.

"The entire ballroom is agog," Valentina finally said after she'd finished ogling herself. "What in the hell is Phillip Grayson doing here?" she nearly spat.

Sophie frowned. "I'm certain I do not know," she answered quietly. There. That much was true. Long ago, she'd taken to telling Valentina as little as possible. The woman usually found a way to use Sophie's words against her. Which was one of many reasons Sophie and Phillip hadn't announced their plans to marry before he left for the Continent with the army three years ago.

Valentina turned to stare at Sophie and crossed her arms over her chest. She arched a dark brow over a catlike eye. "What did you say to him?"

"Nothing," Sophie replied. "He ignored me." There. That was true, and it gave Valentina little to criticize.

Anger flashed in Valentina's eyes. "I wouldn't have blamed you if you told him to go straight to hell. The man has just put a serious cramp in our plans for your marriage."

Sophie's brows snapped together. As usual, Valentina was only worried about herself. If Sophie was no longer engaged to a man who would be a duke, Valentina would no longer be connected to the illustrious Harlowe name. But her step-mother's words caused a lump to form in Sophie's throat. She hadn't thought of it till now, but the gossipmongers would think the same thing Valentina had. That Sophie had confronted Phillip because he'd arrived out of nowhere to take away her chance at being a duchess. She leaned back against the nearest wall, wanting to slide down it and disappear into the floorboards.

"I must speak to Lord Hillsdale," Valentina continued, crossing her arms over her chest and narrowing her eyes once more.

"What does Lord Hillsdale have to do with it?" Sophie replied, frowning. Though an actual helpful thought crossed her mind this time...Valentina's assumption was convenient. If the woman believed Sophie was only angry at Phillip because he'd ruined her betrothal, it would keep Valentina from asking too many questions at least.

Valentina shrugged. "Hillsdale is the authority on titles and lineage in Parliament. He'll know what to do."

Sophie shook her head, the frown still plastered to her face. "He may be the authority, but I'm not certain there's much he can do. Phillip Grayson is the rightful Duke of Harlowe...and he's obviously very much alive."

Valentina waved an elegant, white-gloved hand in the air as if dismissing Sophie's logic. "There must be *some* recourse."

Sophie's frown deepened. Good heavens. Valentina was making no sense. The shock from knowing her stepdaughter would no longer be a duchess had to be addling her brain. Sophie lifted her dark-blue skirts. "I'm going back out. If I stay away too long, it will only make the gossip worse."

"Of course. Of course. Let's go," Valentina replied, lifting her skirts to follow Sophie from the room.

Sophie squared her shoulders and took a deep breath before pulling open the door. Phillip was back. Her best dream and her worst nightmare had just collided into one awful experience she still couldn't quite believe had actually happened. She took a first forceful step into the corridor. She would march back into the ballroom and just dare anyone to say anything to her face.

Including Phillip Grayson.

CHAPTER THREE

Phillip made the rounds through the whisper-filled ballroom, smiling and nodding to the people he used to know—the people who were staring at him now as if he were a specter risen from the grave. Thea had been invaluable earlier, touching his arm and pulling him back from the terror that had enveloped him after hearing the loud crash in the ballroom. Unexpected noises did that to him sometimes, catapulted him back to the battlefield and made him freeze, unable to speak.

Unfortunately, he'd returned to his senses only in time to see Sophie marching away from him.

Thea had quickly informed him of what precisely had happened, and Phillip sorely regretted their first meeting upon his return had been marked by the ghosts of his past coming back to haunt him. But wasn't that why Sophie deserved better? Still, he had to speak to her in private. He had to make it better. He could never make it right.

After Thea had snapped him back to reality, Phillip had pasted a smile on his face, and pretended as if his temporary lapse and the brief encounter with Sophie had never happened. It was the way of their set, was it not? To keep a stiff upper lip, carry on. He'd been skilled in hiding his emotions since the day he was born.

"Well, Your Grace. Are you ever going to tell us who that young lady was and why she looked as if she wanted to step on your foot?" Thea asked from beside him as Phillip walked around the room with the couple.

"Yes, Harlowe. Care to explain what *that* was about?" Clayton added, arching a brow.

Phillip rubbed his forehead. He could not avoid giving his friends an explanation. It surprised him that Thea had taken *this* long to ask, actually. Directly after the incident, both Lord and Lady Clayton had kept smiles plastered on their faces, too. Phillip didn't have to explain to his friends that the best way to draw the least attention to the matter was to act as if it was nothing. Awkward though it might be.

Phillip sighed and spoke under his breath so only Clayton and Thea could hear. "That was Miss Sophia Payton, and if she *had* slapped me, I would have deserved it."

"Ah, *that* was Sophie," Thea replied knowingly. "I might have guessed."

Phillip didn't hear more of his friends' replies. A man bumped into him. *Too close.* The room began to spin. Phillip glanced up to see the glaring chandeliers and then down at the floor to see the scores of shoes and slippers all around him. For the second time that night, sweat beaded on his brow. The room closed in on him.

Thea touched his sleeve again, pulling him back into the moment. *Breathe in. Breathe out.* He forced himself to concentrate on each second. *Three. Two. One.*

Just as Phillip had gained control again, a middle-aged man dressed entirely in dark brown broke away from the crowd and came striding up to them. The man wiped his forehead with a cream-colored handkerchief and stared at

Phillip with an obvious mixture of shock and horror. Phillip pressed his lips together. He supposed he must become accustomed to such stares.

Clayton bowed to the man. "Good evening, Lord Vining. May I introduce you to the Duke of Harlowe?"

Vining promptly bowed to Phillip.

"Your Grace," Clayton continued. "May I present Viscount Vining?"

Phillip nodded to Vining. Clayton knew everyone. The man was the consummate politician. Meanwhile, Phillip had no memory of Lord Vining.

"You're...you're Phillip Grayson?" Lord Vining said as he continued to dab at his wet forehead with the handkerchief. It was spoken as a question, but Phillip instinctively realized the man already knew who he was.

"I am," Phillip replied, studying the man's red face.

"We, er, we thought you were... Well, this is quite awkward, but..." Lord Vining glanced around uneasily.

"You thought I was dead," Phillip replied, smiling calmly at the man whose face was so mottled Phillip was beginning to worry about his health.

"Well, yes," the man said, tugging the handkerchief tight between both hands.

Phillip nodded. "Although my enemy failed to eliminate me on the battlefield, I'm quite aware that news didn't make it home."

Clayton attempted to hide his smile.

Still quite ruddy, Lord Vining continued, "Are you aware that your...I suppose he would be your cousin...has claimed the title?"

"Yes." Phillip nodded. "My first cousin, Hugh. I am *well* aware."

Just then, another man materialized at Vining's side. He put a hand on the viscount's shoulder and patted it. "Good evening, Your Grace," he said smoothly, bowing to Phillip. "It's a pleasure to see you again. I daresay a great, though certainly *unexpected*, pleasure." The man was tall and balding, with an obsequious smile. He bowed again. "Lord Hillsdale," he said by way of introduction.

Phillip nodded in reply. "A pleasure, Lord Hillsdale."

From beside him, Clayton cleared his throat and whispered to Phillip, "Hillsdale is the man in Parliament who handles matters of titles and inheritance."

"Ah, so *you're* the man responsible for handing over my title to my cousin?" Phillip asked, addressing his remark to Lord Hillsdale with a tight smile.

"Mistakes happen, Your Grace," Hillsdale replied smoothly, taking the jibe in stride.

Phillip eyed the older man carefully. A bit of a paunch. Gray in his beard. Far too friendly. From his conversations with Malcolm over the years, Phillip knew that once one became a duke, one had all sorts of new would-be friends to choose from. Hillsdale struck him as a social climber.

"We'll...we'll need to... We must get this sorted," Lord Vining injected, still red and dabbing at the underside of his wet chin.

"All in due time," Hillsdale said, his unctuous grin widening as he addressed Phillip. "Not to worry. I'll send a note round next week and you'll come to Whitehall to discuss it."

Clayton stepped forward. "Yes, well, until then, we'll continue to refer to His Grace here as the Duke of Harlowe. I've known Phillip since he was a child, and I can vouch for his identity. He *is* the rightful duke."

"Of course, of course," Hillsdale replied. "We'll get to the bottom of the matter." He waved his hand in the air, as if dismissing the subject.

"This is quite unusual," Lord Vining added, tugging at his

cravat as if the thing might strangle him. "Quite unusual indeed."

"What's unusual," Phillip replied, keeping his face perfectly blank, "is that my cousin claimed the title so soon after my brother's death, before verifying *mine.*"

Lord Vining audibly gulped. His beady eyes watered. "It was announced in the papers. You died in the battle of *Morales de Toro.*"

"Now, Vining, that's quite enough," Lord Hillsdale sternly interjected, frowning openly at the shorter man. "Where are your manners? We must welcome His Grace back to town properly. Care for a drink, *Your Grace?*"

Phillip completely ignored Hillsdale's words. He arched a brow and addressed Lord Vining directly. "As you can see, I did not die at *Morales de Toro*, my lord," he replied, the barest hint of a smile on his face, "regardless of what the papers printed." *Hmm.* This was more amusing than he'd thought it would be. Of course Phillip still didn't relish the fact that the entire ballroom was talking about him behind their hands, fans, and handkerchiefs, and he'd have to face Sophie again eventually, but flustering this blowhard was nothing but diverting.

"Well, yes. Of course. I can see that now," Lord Vining choked out. "As Hillsdale said, we'll just sort it out, er... later."

"That sounds like a perfect plan," Clayton replied, smiling tightly at the man.

"What about that drink? May I get you something?" Lord Hillsdale offered again, obsequious smile still firmly in place.

"No, thank you, my lord," Phillip replied. "Now, if you'll both excuse us. My friends and I are off to make the rounds."

"Of course, of course," Hillsdale replied, stepping aside and splaying out one arm as if to guide Phillip's course away from him.

Phillip, Clayton, and Thea brushed past Vining and Hillsdale, walked for a bit, and came to a stop in the middle of the ballroom. The entire company still staring at them, Phillip felt like a statue in a square that had just been revealed. Good God. How long would this last? He supposed he owed the *ton* a good long look. According to Grimaldi and Bell, it was important that everyone saw it was indeed him. Alive and well.

"Vining is a lackwit," Clayton said under his breath as they pretended to be enjoying themselves. Fortunately, none of the other partygoers had the gumption to approach them, so they were quite safe to talk without being overheard.

Phillip nodded at that pronouncement. "He seemed quite taken aback by my presence."

"I thought he was going to rip that handkerchief to shreds," Thea added with a sly smile.

"What about Hillsdale?" Phillip asked.

Clayton lifted his brows. "As I mentioned, it's his function to ensure titles are inherited appropriately," the viscount replied. "No doubt he wonders whether he'll be sacked for this mistake. Not to mention he's a notorious bootlick to anyone who has a more prestigious title than he does. I'm certain he wants to make fast friends with you."

Phillip had to chuckle. "That explains why I don't remember ever meeting him before, when I was merely a second son, but I cannot possibly be the first nobleman to return from the grave."

"Certainly not," Clayton replied with a grin. "But you're probably the first one on Hillsdale's watch. He'll be calling on you first thing next week to discuss it further. As I recall, he played a large role in helping your cousin claim the title. He'll want to put it to rights immediately with as little fanfare as possible."

"Good. So do I. I look forward to his visit," Phillip replied.

"I only hope he doesn't bring Vining with him. The man will perspire himself into a puddle all over your carpets, Clayton."

"Yes, let's avoid that unpleasant outcome," Thea added with a laugh.

Phillip glanced around. He was trying not to study the ballroom with too careful an eye. But where had Sophie got off to? Had she left the ball? He wouldn't blame her if she had. But running away was unlike her. Sophie was head-strong and brave. But he hadn't mistaken the tears in her eyes that he'd seen just before the crash had stolen his equi-librium. He owed her an explanation. However unsatisfying it might be.

"I suppose we should continue to make the rounds," Clayton said, glancing about the ballroom in search of their next stop.

"No, actually," Phillip replied in a firm voice. "I need to speak with Miss Payton alone, and I need your help."

CHAPTER FOUR

The eyes of the entire ballroom were on her. Sophie could feel them boring into her, taking in her every movement. All talking had ceased as she'd made her way back into the ballroom. She'd held her head high and continued to walk on shaky legs as group after group noticed her and fell silent, watching as she and Valentina made their way unerringly back to their small set.

When they arrived, Sophie kept a falsely pleasant look on her face as she pretended to be listening to Valentina's friends' conversation, which was conspicuously, yet thankfully, *not* about Phillip. If it had been about him, she would have had to make her excuses and go, even if every person in the ballroom guessed why she was leaving.

Sophie couldn't help but let her gaze wander across the ballroom. She couldn't find Phillip anywhere. Where was he? He couldn't possibly have left already, could he?

Beside her, she could practically feel Valentina's uneasiness. Her stepmother had wandered off and was now doing her best to get Lord Hillsdale's attention, even though the man stood across the room in a group with others. Valentina clearly wanted to speak to him privately, but Lord Hillsdale hadn't noticed her waving her arm at him. Sophie would laugh at her stepmother's foolish antics if the whole affair wasn't still making her own nerves jangle. Where was Phillip? And for that matter, where was Hugh? He should have arrived by now.

A quarter hour had passed by the time Valentina finally got Lord Hillsdale off alone. She'd been forced to go pluck him out of the crowd, while Sophie was left to stare awkwardly about, smiling noncommittally at her stepmother's boring friends. Normally, Sophie would have a full dance card, but tonight, *no one* had asked her to dance. Apparently, watching her was more entertaining than dancing with her.

"Miss Payton?" came a bright female voice, interrupting Sophie from her thoughts.

Sophie turned to see Lady Clayton standing behind her. Lady Clayton was pretty with dark hair and gray eyes, and she was wearing a gorgeous, high-waisted, lavender gown that complimented her lovely figure.

"Lady Clayton?" Sophia replied, curtsying and somewhat surprised to be addressed by the woman. What could Lady Clayton possibly want with her? They had never spoken before. And the woman had arrived with Phillip, which made dread curdle in Sophie's middle.

"I was hoping you'd take a turn about the room with me," Lady Clayton said, a friendly smile on her face.

Warning bells sounded in Sophie's head. No good would come of taking a turn around the room with Lady Clayton. Sophie knew it and yet, only a moment later, she found herself agreeing, based solely on the fact that she could not find an adequate excuse to say no.

The slightly older woman slipped an arm through Sophie's and led her away. They kept to the perimeter of the large room, while Sophie made a game of staring through anyone they encountered, as if they didn't exist. She didn't want to see the censure in their eyes. Or the curiosity in their gazes.

"Thank you for walking with me," Lady Clayton began.

"This is about Phillip, isn't it?" Sophie asked. She'd never been one for meaningless chatter. She preferred to get straight to a matter.

Lady Clayton continued both smiling and walking as she replied, "Yes. Yes, it is."

"Well, then. You might as well tell me precisely what you intend to say. I'd prefer it that way," Sophie replied, her heart hammering in her chest.

Lady Clayton looked at Sophie from the corners of her eyes and her careful smile turned into a friendly grin. "I like you. I've always admired a young lady who gets to the point. I prefer it myself."

"Go ahead," Sophie prodded, still feeling as if she might cast up her accounts at any moment. She couldn't bear the suspense, wondering what Lady Clayton would say.

Lady Clayton took a deep breath. "There is much you don't know about where Phillip has been, what he's been through and—"

Sophie clenched her jaw. "On the contrary, I don't know *a thing* about where Phillip has been," she clarified.

Lady Clayton nodded. "Yes, well, the fact is that he would very much like to speak with you alone, and I've come to ask if you will agree to do so."

"Alone?" *Alone with Phillip?* More alarm bells sounded in Sophie's head. "How would we speak alone?"

Lady Clayton kept her gaze trained straight ahead and that pleasant smile pasted on her lips. "Not half an hour past, my husband escorted the duke to Lord Cranberry's billiards room. They are even now taking in a game with some of the other gentlemen."

"And?" Sophie asked, frowning. What did a game of billiards have to do with her and Phillip speaking alone?

"When that game is through," Lady Clayton continued calmly, "Phillip plans to go to the north salon downstairs. It's empty. Or it was a few minutes ago."

Sophie sucked in her breath. She was quickly beginning to understand. Lady Clayton had come to fetch her. "I see. And you want me to meet Phillip there?"

Another nod. "I will go with you in case you're seen. You'll only have to tell your Mama you need some fresh air or something."

Sophie glanced over at Valentina, who was engaged in a hand-gesture-filled exchange with Lord Hillsdale near a potted palm in the corner. "She's my *step*mother," Sophie replied in a low voice.

"Ah, I see," Lady Clayton replied.

Sophie considered the viscountess's words for a few moments while they continued to walk. She wasn't certain why she was contemplating taking up Lady Clayton on her offer, but she was. She was more than contemplating it, actually. She'd already decided she would go. Just like that. She had to. She couldn't help it. Phillip had ignored her earlier and now he wanted to speak to her alone? Why? What had changed in the last hour? And more importantly, what could the man possibly say to make it all right? He'd let her believe he was *dead*, for God's sake.

"If I go now, I believe Valentina won't notice," Sophie heard herself reply.

"Excellent," came Lady Clayton's response. "I'll just drift off into the crowd as if we're done speaking. I'll go out the side door by the orchestra. You go out the main doors. I'll meet you at the head of the staircase in a few minutes."

Sophie nodded and swallowed hard as Lady Clayton released her arm and drifted away. Another quick glance at

Valentina told Sophie her stepmother was still occupied with Lord Hillsdale. It was now or never. Sophie lifted her skirts and made straight for the doors. Oh, people would be watching. And wondering where she'd gone. But none of them would be bold enough to follow her...she hoped.

As she hurried out the door, Lady Clayton's words played themselves through Sophie's mind again. She'd cut off the lady, but she'd said something like, "There is much you don't know about what Phillip's been through." That had been a strange choice of words. What could Lady Clayton have possibly meant by it? Besides, if Phillip had been through something difficult, so had Sophie. She'd been forced to believe the man she loved was *dead*, of all horrible things. Even so, she couldn't keep from wondering...what *had* he been through? Sophie shook her head to clear it of such thoughts. Sympathy for Phillip was the last thing she wanted to feel just before she was about to see him again.

As promised, Lady Clayton was standing at the top of the staircase when Sophie arrived minutes later.

"Thank you for coming," Lady Clayton breathed, before turning toward the stairs. The two made their way silently down to the salon and stood in front of the imposing double doors. Pausing, Sophie pressed her hand to her middle once again. There was still every chance she might cast up her accounts tonight, and seeing Phillip again just might be the reason. She *must* remember why she was angry, or she would end up in a puddle at his feet within minutes.

Lady Clayton pushed open the door to reveal Phillip standing at the far end of the room, staring out the darkened windows. A few candles placed on tables throughout lit the space enough for Sophie to make out his form. He was tall and blond and so handsome her knees were weak. Her heart twisted in her chest. Seeing him again was sweet agony.

A memory flashed through her mind of the night before

26

Phillip had gone off to war. The last time she'd seen him. They were standing on the balcony of the Miltons' town house. A ball was in full swing in the ballroom behind them. A breeze had lifted the roguish lock of hair that fell over his green eyes, and he'd promised her forever that night. She'd obviously been a fool. But she was older and wiser now. She was no longer a fool.

Phillip turned to her. "Sophie," he breathed.

She caught her breath, wishing she had something to hold on to. An anchor. She needed an anchor. Hearing her name on his lips nearly wrecked her. Why couldn't he have looked at her like this earlier? Or simply looked at her at all? She crossed her arms tightly over her chest, and forced a glare to her face, hoping her countenance told him she'd like nothing more than to slap him. Perhaps even make it a punch.

The door closed behind her and for an awful moment, Sophie realized Lady Clayton meant to leave them alone. Nearly panicking, Sophie stepped back and ripped open the door. "You must stay with me, Lady Clayton," she said in a voice that was far more high-pitched than she'd meant it to be. "You promised to. For propriety's sake."

As excuses went, it was particularly rubbish. If Sophie gave a whit about propriety, she never would have confronted the newly returned duke in the middle of the Cranberrys' ball. But panic was a cruel master, making her say anything to get what she wanted, and right now what she wanted was another person in the room while Phillip said whatever he had to say. The odds of her slapping him, kissing him, or melting on his boots were greatly reduced with another occupant in this room.

After a brief nod from Phillip—which Sophie did not miss—Lady Clayton quickly complied. The viscountess stepped back into the salon and closed the door, pulling the knobs together and holding them behind her back, presumably to ensure no one else attempted to enter.

"Your gown...you look...beautiful," Phillip began. Was it her imagination or did his voice quaver? *That* was unexpected. And Phillip sounded...almost shy. A bit unsure of himself. That was unlike him too, though she found it... adorable. Unwanted adorableness at the moment, but adorable just the same.

"Thank you," she replied, a polite reflex. Was she really doing this? Was she really standing here talking to Phillip again? The man she'd dreamed of nightly for so long? Was this happening or was it a fever dream?

"Thea says you looked as if you wanted to step on my foot earlier. Do you?" he asked, the side of his lips tugging up in an all-too-familiar half-smile that made her heart flip.

She opened her mouth to speak but shut it again, not trusting herself to say the proper thing. She'd had to become careful over the last year. She'd had to learn to speak without saying what she truly felt. Had to learn to pretend to be alive when she'd felt as if she'd died along with Phillip on that battlefield. Only he hadn't died, had he? He was standing here now, asking her if she wanted to step on his foot. Her entire reality had turned upside down in the span of one ball.

"If you did, it would be nothing more than what I deserve," Phillip continued, coming to stand just a pace away from her.

"You deserve much worse," Sophie replied, trying her best not to let the sadness seep into her voice. Anger. Only anger tonight. But she could smell him. And the scent of his familiar cologne made her clench her jaw, made tears well in her eyes again.

"We don't have long," he said. "No doubt there's a gaggle of people already looking for both of us."

She lifted her chin. There. There was the confident, in-control Phillip she remembered. But he'd been vulnerable for a moment, and she would never forget it. "Fine. Say what you must," she replied, matching his brisk tone.

Phillip glanced at Lady Clayton before turning his attention back to Sophie. His gaze met and held hers. "I'm sorry, Sophia," he whispered, but with a sincerity that made her want to sob. "*That's* what I want to say."

"Sorry for what?" She forced the words past her lips.

He arched a brow, giving her a look that clearly said, *isn't it obvious?*

Her anger stoked, Sophie drew up her shoulders. She would be damned if she let him get away with a simple, "I'm sorry." The man needed to explain himself. Immediately. Not to mention, he'd called her Sophia. Why? He'd always called her Sophie before. Why was he being so formal?

Her nostrils flared as she sucked in a deep breath. "That's all you have to say to me?" Her voice was sharp.

His face was a mask. "I owe you an apology. I gave you one."

All hints of sadness gone. Red-hot anger flashed before her eyes. How could he be so nonchalant about this? He'd called her in here for *this*? Not good enough. Nowhere near. "Of course you owe me an apology. But I expected one with some sort of explanation for why you've apparently been pretending to be *dead* for the last year," she shot back at him.

Phillip straightened his shoulders and smoothed a hand down his coat front. "I cannot tell you that." His voice was solemn but resolute.

"Unacceptable," she said evenly, but her nostrils still flared.

"Please, Sophie," he whispered.

And *there* was the Sophie. At least he'd given her that. That, coupled with his familiar scent, were the only two things letting her know she was sane. This was Phillip, after all, not some imposter. She knew it as certain as she knew her own name. She tossed back her head, not caring that a lock of her curly hair bounced to her shoulder. "Please, what? What can you possibly say to make this all right?" Sophie glanced at Lady Clayton. The acting door guard shifted uncomfortably on both feet, and stared at her slippers, obviously wishing she was elsewhere.

Phillip glanced at Lady Clayton too. Was he embarrassed to have his friend hear this? Good!

"I can leave," Lady Clayton offered in a far-too-eager voice.

"No, Lady Clayton," Sophie replied. "I want a witness to whatever outlandish tale *His Grace* here is going to spin."

"Oh, dear." Lady Clayton glanced down at her feet again and rocked back and forth on her heels, biting her lip.

"It's fine, Thea. Stay," Phillip added. Oh, so he was on a first name basis with Lady Clayton? *That* was interesting. Apparently, *she'd* known he wasn't dead.

"Oh, but first," Sophie said, irony dripping from her voice. "Let's tell Lady Clayton here the details. The things she needs to know. Or have you already done that?"

Lady Clayton glanced up. Her face turned pink, and she looked as if she wanted to sprint from the room.

"No, of course not," Phillip replied, quietly.

Sophie couldn't feel sorry for him. He deserved this. He deserved to be embarrassed in front of his friend for the mistakes he'd made. He deserved to have to answer right here and now for what he'd done. Sophie crossed her arms over her chest even tighter and walked around Phillip in a wide circle.

"It was three years ago," Sophie began. "I was just out. I fell head over heels in love with this blackguard." She pointed her chin toward Phillip.

Lady Clayton nodded and cleared her throat.

"And I offered for you," Phillip added just as quietly.

Lady Clayton's eyes widened momentarily. Apparently, he'd been telling the truth about not telling Lady Clayton about them. Not everything, at least.

"No. No. No, you didn't," Sophie clarified, pointing a finger in the air. "You *nearly* offered for me."

Phillip nodded.

Lady Clayton's eyes went back to their normal size.

"You said you *would* offer for me as soon as you returned from war. *If* you returned from war," Sophie continued.

"Yes," Phillip allowed. "That's true."

Sophie's throat ached with unshed tears of anger and sadness. "And I wrote to you nearly every day."

"Yes." His jaw was clenched. Good. She'd affected him. She knew she had.

"And you wrote to me too, declaring your undying love. Did you not?" It felt good. Saying all of this aloud. No matter what was going on with Phillip now. He could never take away the truth of their past together. She would always have that much.

"I did," Phillip allowed.

Sophie battled the tears that welled in her eyes. She would win, blast it. She would. Or she would die trying. "And here you are, *Your Grace*," she sneered. "Or is that title not officially yours?"

"Not yet," he replied woodenly. "I've only just returned." He glanced at Lady Clayton again, who gave him a pleading stare, one that made Sophie wonder what exactly the viscountess knew. But no matter. Sophie was about to finish this conversation. After all these months of pretending to be alive, it felt glorious to feel something again, anything. Even if it was anger. And as long as she was feeling something, she intended to have her say.

Sophie stopped walking around Phillip and braced her

gloved hands on her hips. "Here you are. Did you call me here to make good on your promise? Are you offering for me now?"

Phillip's head snapped to the side, and he met her gaze, his eyes hard as emeralds. "I saw this morning's paper. It appears I am too late."

CHAPTER FIVE

Phillip shot up in bed, covered in sweat. He hadn't had a full night's sleep since the battle. When he drifted off, he would hear gunshots and screams, smell blood and gunpowder, and hear the cries of men and horses. He remembered it all. Things he never should have seen. Things no one should ever have to see. The memories haunted his nights. Tonight did not differ from all the others.

It took several moments to orient himself. *Three. Two. One.* He was secure in the dark, cool bedchamber at Clayton's town house in London. He wasn't on the Continent. He wasn't at war. His breathing finally steadied, and he pushed off the covers, stood, and paced over to the window to look out on the London street below. It always helped to see a landmark, to realize he was truly safe.

London seemed like a completely different town now. It was no longer the place he'd lived most of his years. The last time he'd been here, he'd been a pampered nobleman, the offspring of a duke. He'd attended balls and parties and had been welcomed into the finest clubs. Now he felt like an outsider. Like someone who knew a horrible secret he couldn't share with anyone else.

He rubbed the back of his neck while his father's words rang in his head. "You'll be an officer in His Majesty's Army, Phillip. That's the job for a second son." His father had always been preoccupied with how everything looked. Appearance and reputation were everything to him. Phillip had wanted to be a scholar. He'd wanted to go to Europe and study the history, architecture, and culture of different lands. But he hadn't even attempted to tell his father as much. The former duke would never have agreed to his second son being anything other than a war hero. Duty was more important than anything. Wasn't that what he'd been raised to believe?

And Phillip had done his duty. It had nearly cost him his life. It had nearly cost him his sanity. It did cost him... Phillip pushed away thoughts of Sophie.

Father would hate to know what had become of his precious title. Not only was Malcolm dead, but Cousin Hugh (the only son of Father's only brother) was named Duke of Harlowe. Father had detested Hugh. The old man had to be turning in his grave.

Phillip had done his duty as a soldier, and now that he was back, he'd perform another important duty...he'd see that honor and dignity were restored to the Harlowe title and lands. He would take his rightful place as the duke. But first, he would find out precisely what had happened to his brother. Nothing was more important. Not regaining the title immediately. Or explaining to his former love why he hadn't been able to tell her he wasn't dead.

And there was a good reason for that. At first, he'd been recovering, too ill to write, too ill to do anything. He'd nearly died from an infection of the blood. Then, when he was finally feeling like a human again, he'd learned that Malcolm had died. And Bell had been adamant. Until they learned who was behind Malcolm's murder, *everyone* was suspected. *No one* could know that Phillip was alive.

Phillip owed Bell his life. The marquess had been the one responsible for getting an injured Phillip off the ship from the Continent and moved to Clayton's country estate before anyone became the wiser that he was alive, to give him the best chance of recovering in peace. Bell had arrived at Clayton's estate last year for a series of visits with a handful of theories, not the least of which had been that Sophie herself might well be involved in the murder. Apparently, Sophie had often been seen in Cousin Hugh's company soon after the man had arrived in London and claimed the title.

Phillip had waved off the notion of Sophie's involvement as ludicrous. The lovely, unconventional girl he'd met at a Society dinner wasn't capable of hurting a gadfly, let alone taking part in the murder of a grown man. Phillip *knew* it. But he also knew that Sophie was impulsive and could very well unintentionally tell the wrong person he was alive and ruin everything. Or she would attempt to visit him, and his secret would be out. No. It had been best to keep her in the dark until Malcolm's murderer was firmly behind bars. He'd made that decision knowing full well that one day he would have to account for it with Sophie.

Phillip moved away from the window to the small desk in his bedchamber. He pulled open a drawer and pulled out a dirty, blood-stained letter. Sophie's last letter, the one he'd had near his heart the moment he'd nearly died. It had got him through some very dark days.

He'd written her too once he'd been well enough. He'd written to tell her he was alive. Only he'd never posted the letter. Instead, he'd kept it under lock and key in a box at Clayton's estate, tortured by the fact that one day he'd return and be forced to see the look on her face when she realized he'd deceived her.

Phillip put the letter back in the drawer and moved back over to the window. He braced his forearm against the wall and rested his forehead upon the cool glass. He let out a deep groan. The moment of reckoning had been last night. Sophie had never looked more beautiful. Or angrier. And he'd never seen her angry before. When he saw her in the salon, he could hardly tear his gaze from her. He'd been disappointed that she'd insisted on keeping Thea in the room, but he had no right to argue. Not only was there propriety to consider, but Sophie clearly hadn't wanted to be left alone with him, a decision she was entitled to make.

After Bell had informed him not two days ago that Sophie's betrothal to Hugh was to be announced in the paper this morning, Phillip had felt physically ill. Hugh was high on the list of people whom Bell suspected could have been involved in Malcolm's murder, which made Sophie seem even more suspicious to the marquess. But Phillip had no doubts. Not Sophie. Never Sophie. There had to be a good explanation for her engagement to Hugh. Phillip had intended to ask her last night. Only there hadn't been time, because Sophie had asked a question of her own, "Are you offering for me now?"

She'd been mocking him because she was angry. He could see the hurt in her eyes as she'd asked the question. His answer had been quiet and vicious, filled with all the hurt and anger in his own heart. He hadn't been able to stop the words from leaving his mouth. "It appears I am too late."

Her face had fallen, and he'd seen her swallow a lump in her throat. Tears still quivering in her eyes, she'd turned away and rushed from the room. Thea had followed her, while Phillip had cursed under his breath. It had been a deuced awful thing to say, and he knew it. He had no excuse. And now he had no answers.

Damn it. Why *had* she become engaged to Hugh? Why Hugh? Phillip could understand that she'd moved on—after all, she thought he was dead—but *why Hugh?* Phillip refused to believe Bell was right, that Sophie was somehow connected to his brother's death. But that didn't stop Bell from trying to convince him. They'd had the same conversation at least a half dozen times.

"Miss Payton obviously saw a chance to become a duchess and took it," Bell would say.

"That makes no sense," Phillip always countered. "When I promised for her, I wasn't a duke. Malcolm had been quite alive and well."

"Unless…" Bell replied, allowing the sentence to drift off, knowing they both understood what he refused to voice. That Sophie may have been planning to murder Malcolm all along.

Beyond ludicrous, as far as Phillip was concerned. He usually stormed off, refusing to talk to the marquess about the subject again. Though it was only a matter of time before it came up once more.

"Sophie," Phillip whispered under his breath. "What's happened to us?" A memory floated through his brain. The memory of the night he'd met Sophie at the Remingtons' dinner party. She'd been out on the verandah where he'd gone for a bit of peace, only to find a beautiful young woman wearing a simple white gown and matching slippers with daisies entwined in her unruly dark hair, who eagerly spoke, asking him a host of inappropriate questions, all while seeming to be the happiest, brightest soul he'd ever encountered. And being the realist, stoic soul that *he* was, he'd been immediately drawn to her light, her verve, her uncomplicated way of looking at the world. He wished he could be that carefree.

After introducing herself with the most delightfully awkward curtsy Phillip had ever witnessed, he'd been doing his damnedest to hide his smile when she cocked her head to the side and demanded, "Why are you out here? Don't you care for parties?"

"I detest them," he'd replied somberly.

She'd blinked at him, truly curious. "Why?"

He'd shrugged. "Too many people. Too much noise."

"Well," she'd replied with an adorable little shrug of her own, "I completely agree with you about the noise. It's an infernal racket in there. But I do adore balls. Where else can you find so much ridiculousness in one spot? I mean, Lady Cranberry is wearing a headful of feathers. Feathers! Multiple! She looks like a daft bird. And *everyone* in there takes themself soooo very seriously," she continued, lowering her voice and drawing out her words. "I just escaped Lord Holt telling everyone about a rock he brought back from Greece. A rock! Can you imagine?" she'd continued with a bright smile.

Phillip had turned to her, eyes narrowed. "What sort of rock?"

"Oh, no!" She'd placed the back of her hand to her forehead in a mock display of distress. "Please don't tell me you're a rock *aficionado*. I'm afraid we cannot be friends if you like to speak at length about rocks."

He'd laughed out loud at that, and she'd grinned unrepentantly back at him.

"So ridiculousness…*that's* the reason to attend a ball, eh?" he'd ventured.

Sophie had shrugged. "That and the ever-present possibility of a scandal. Though, honestly, I prefer the ridiculous."

Phillip had laughed yet again, completely enchanted by

the young woman who had such a unique way of looking at their world, a world which he merely found exceedingly boring most of the time.

Later that night, on the way back home from the ball, he'd realized how rarely he laughed—couldn't remember the *last* time he'd laughed, in fact—and how he'd never considered just how truly ridiculous balls were. Miss Sophia Payton was right. And she was delightful.

Before she'd disappeared back into the brightly lit ballroom, she'd announced that they should be fast friends, provided he promised to never discuss rocks with her. He'd quickly agreed.

Over the next several months, he'd found himself looking for her in every crowd. They spent more and more time together at each event they attended. They continued their unconventional friendship throughout the Season, and it wasn't until just before he was about to leave for the Continent—for the war—that Phillip realized he'd become hopelessly in love with her without even trying.

He'd wanted to drop to one knee that night on the Miltons' balcony and declare himself. Only he knew that would be selfish of him. Sophie was a young, beautiful woman. He did not know if he'd survive. He couldn't ask her to wait for him. He couldn't ask her to possibly grieve for him at such a young age. But he *had* promised her that if she did wait, he would offer for her the moment he returned. That had been three years ago.

And now Sophie was engaged to Hugh. Not that he could blame her for being engaged. She'd thought he was dead. Phillip scrubbed a hand through his hair and then over his face. How had their love affair, so promising and innocent once, turned into the awkward meeting they'd had in the Cranberrys' salon tonight and Sophie running from the room in tears? *Was* she in love with Hugh? Phillip's heart refused to believe that. Hugh was lazy, rude, crass, and arrogant. There was no way Sophie would have chosen him for herself. But everything was still so unclear. He knew one thing, however. He had to learn the truth about his brother's death as quickly as possible.

Which meant his first order of business would be working with Bell to investigate Malcolm's death. There were many questions, so many questions Phillip didn't yet know the answers to. But he knew one thing for certain...*anyone* involved in his brother's death, and anyone who might hurt Sophie, would pay.

CHAPTER SIX

"**V**alentina, please sit down. You're wearing a hole in the rug," Sophie said as her stepmother passed by her seat for what felt like the hundredth time that morning. The three of them were in Papa's gold salon, where Valentina had just finished reading the paper and had turned it over to Papa with a disgusted grunt.

Papa was sitting on the sofa busily studying the Society pages, while Valentina continued to walk back and forth in front of him, her eyes narrowed and a sour expression on her face. If you asked Sophie, pacing was a completely useless endeavor.

"I cannot sit down," Valentina replied, turning again with a sharp flip of her bright pink skirts. Her fists were clenched at her sides, and she was nearly shaking with nerves. "Your entire future...*our family's* entire future is at stake here, Sophia, and you act as if nothing has happened."

Last night in the lady's retiring room at the Cranberrys' ball, Valentina had seemed unconcerned by Phillip's return. This morning, she was nearly unstrung, and Sophie suspected her stepmother's conversation with Lord Hillsdale was the reason for her change in temperament.

"What can we do about it?" Sophie replied, wanting to sigh, but not daring to. Valentina didn't take kindly to her sighs. "Worrying won't solve the problem," Sophie pointed out.

Valentina glared at her. "Do you hear this, Roger?" she asked Papa, plunking her hands on her hips.

Sophie lowered her gaze to roll her eyes. Another reaction Valentina didn't care for, and whenever Valentina didn't like something that Sophie said or did, she complained to Papa.

"I'm trying to read, dearest," Papa replied, in his appeasing-Valentina voice, still intently studying the paper.

"Well, read faster," Valentina snapped. "This problem will not solve itself."

Sophie turned her attention back to the horticulture book she was pretending to read. She didn't care a whit about horticulture, but tending a garden *seemed* like a lovely pastime and if she were going to pretend to like something, it might as well be horticulture. Besides, books one didn't care a whit about were the perfect choice of reading material when one could not concentrate.

Sophie had spent a sleepless night in her bed, a bevy of thoughts racing through her mind one after another. They were still racing. She might not be pacing like Valentina, but that didn't mean Sophie wasn't every bit as anxious.

Last night, she and Valentina had ridden home from the Cranberrys' ball in complete silence. For once, her normally overly talkative stepmother didn't say a word. She'd just sat in stony silence, staring out the window, her arms crossed over her chest. That had been Sophie's first clue that whatever Lord Hillsdale had told Valentina hadn't pleased her.

Sophie had been grateful for Valentina's silence. She'd had

her own thoughts to contend with. Besides the dread she always felt in a coach because of the space being so tight and close, a riot of emotions had streamed through her last night, leaving her feeling like a used handkerchief. She wanted to climb into bed and sleep until the Season ended. She wanted to rage against the unfairness of life. She'd wanted to step on Phillip's foot after he'd had the audacity to say, "It appears I am too late," when she'd asked him if he'd intended to offer for her. And why *had* she asked him such an outlandish thing? The words had just spilled from her lips without examination. Her anger had reached a boiling point when she'd remembered that the last words he'd said to her before they parted on the Miltons' balcony—just before he'd gone to war—and they had come back to taunt her last night. "I cannot ask you to wait for me, Sophie, but if you do, I will offer for you the moment I return." Those words ripped at her heart, making a mockery of all her dreams.

She'd been so hurt by his reply last night, she'd run from the salon like a coward. She hated herself for doing that. Lady Clayton had followed her and tried to speak with her, but Sophie had steadfastly refused, asking the viscountess to return to the party without her.

In bed later, however, Sophie had plenty of time to think about what a fool she'd been for being so hurt and angry. After all, she was betrothed to someone else. Phillip's first cousin, no less. She certainly never would have agreed to the engagement if she'd known Phillip was still alive. But *Phillip* didn't know that. The whole thing was maddening. Maddening, dispiriting, and awful. It was all three, and that was all there was to it.

Sophie had always counted herself a positive person. She preferred to be pleasant and look on the brighter side of any issue. But even a positive person was hard-pressed to find the bright side of *this* debacle. What were they to do now?

Any of them? It wasn't as if she could cry off from Hugh and declare her undying love for Phillip. She didn't even know Phillip any longer. Apparently, she never had, if he was the sort of man who would deceive her about something as important as his own *death*. Besides, Phillip hadn't given her any indication that he still felt the same for her. It stood to reason that he did not. A man in love would hardly keep the news of his survival from his beloved. And if that wasn't confusing enough, then there was Hugh.

Hugh had never arrived last night. At first, Sophie hadn't been able to decide if that was a good or a bad thing. After much consideration during the wee hours of the morning, she'd finally decided on good. She couldn't have stood it if she'd had to face *him*, too. Hugh was an odd duck. The man had been pursuing her for some time now, ever since he arrived in town and took up the title last year. Sophie had thought little of him during his first several weeks in town. But somehow, he and Valentina had become thick as thieves, and Valentina had pushed Sophie and Hugh together at every opportunity.

It had ended in Valentina and Papa forcing Sophie to accept Hugh's suit a fortnight ago. And Sophie had agreed, mainly because it was easier to become engaged than to argue with Valentina about it any longer. And if Sophie *were* betrothed, she could at least attend social events without Valentina constantly bringing up the fact that she *wasn't* engaged. With Phillip no longer alive, Sophie cared little about who she was betrothed to. But she had asked both Papa and Valentina about a nice, long engagement. Perhaps she would at least develop a friendship with Hugh. She didn't know him well, and what she did know about him wasn't particularly attractive. Oh, he was a good enough *looking* man, though hardly as handsome as Phillip. But Hugh was arrogant and could be tactless. He was prone to lying to make himself look better. And on more than one occasion she'd heard him be outright ill-mannered to people, usually servants and those he considered beneath him socially.

It wasn't unheard of for a betrothed couple in their set to be as unfamiliar with each other as she and Hugh were, but it certainly was not Sophie's preference. She'd always had her heart set on marrying for love. And she'd believed that Phillip would make that dream come true.

Sophie continued to stare unseeing at the pages of the large book opened on her lap. She didn't want to think about Phillip. Every time she did, it felt as if her heart were in a vise, and she couldn't breathe. Instead, she would focus her thoughts on Hugh. Hugh who made her feel nothing more than mild distaste. She could breathe just fine when thinking about Hugh.

What would Hugh say when he did finally show his face? No doubt he would have a slew of questions for her, beginning with why was she seen talking to his cousin soon after his entrance to the ball last night? What would she tell him? She had told no one about her past with Phillip. Not Valentina or Papa. Valentina wouldn't have been happy. She'd always told Sophie she would be a duchess one day and marrying *the younger brother* of a duke was not the way to go about it. Why her stepmother was so obsessed with the idea of Sophie becoming a duchess, Sophie would never know. Valentina often prattled on about her own missed opportunities and the need to be connected to the 'right' sort of people. Whatever *that* meant.

Sophie hadn't given a toss about being a duchess. All she'd ever wanted was to be loved and love someone completely in return. And she *had* loved Phillip. So much. Her chest ached when she thought about how very much she had loved him. How devastated she'd been the day she'd learned of his death.

But now...now she didn't even know who he was. *Or* where he'd been all these months.

Her emotions were bouncing about. She was angry. She was sad. She was—ecstatic? For one heart-stopping moment when she'd seen Phillip standing there at the front of the ballroom, alive and well, her heart had hammered so hard in her chest she thought she might faint. But she wasn't a fainter, and soul-simmering anger had quickly swept through her, replacing her joy at once more seeing the face she'd loved for so long. It hadn't been a choice, really, the decision to approach him. Her feet had moved of their own accord.

She glanced over at Valentina again. The woman was still pacing and fanning herself so rapidly that Sophie thought the fan might snap in half. Sophie closed her eyes and sank back into her seat, letting the book fall against her chest. Her head was throbbing, and she felt vaguely ill. How in the world would all of this end?

"It says here you must have confronted Phillip Grayson for ruining your chances of becoming a duchess," Papa reported from the sofa, the paper splayed wide in front of his face. "It says you looked quite angry."

Sophie groaned. Valentina had been right. The *ton* had assumed the worst. The thought made Sophie want to growl. She took a deep breath and reminded herself that it would give everyone something to believe, at least. She and Phillip knew the truth, so what did it matter?

"They wonder why Hugh wasn't at the ball last night," Papa reported next. "They guess he may have known that his cousin Phillip was returning."

"Yes," Valentina said, her fan still shaking in her hand, anger simmering in her voice. "I have the same question myself. I intend to ask Hugh the *moment* he arrives."

Sophie's eyes flew open, and she sat up straight, clutching

the book to her chest. "What? Is Hugh coming here?" The throbbing in her head intensified.

Valentina glanced at the clock on the mantel. "He's late. He should be here by now. What could be keeping him?" Her eyes narrowed even further, if that was possible.

Sophie blew out a breath. Knowing Hugh, he was probably hiding. He'd never seemed a brave sort. But the news of his imminent arrival was all Sophie needed to hear. She didn't dare take a chance. She wasn't ready to face Hugh and have an awkward conversation with him. "My head aches," she announced, quickly standing. "I'm going to my bedchamber." She tossed the horticulture book onto the sofa she'd just vacated and started for the door. She had absolutely no intention of going to her bedchamber, but Papa and Valentina didn't need to know that.

"I'll send a maid to fetch you if Hugh wishes to speak to you," Valentina replied haughtily, lifting her nose in the air.

Sophie was glad she was facing the opposite direction so her stepmother couldn't see her roll her eyes at *that* lofty pronouncement. Instead, Sophie hurried toward the door.

She'd barely reached the door when Valentina said to Papa, "I say there's still hope she'll be a duchess yet."

"What?" Sophie wheeled around. What in heaven's name did Valentina mean? She couldn't possibly mean...by marrying *Phillip*, could she? No. No. That couldn't be.

"There's no proof that man was actually Phillip Grayson," Valentina continued, her silver-green eyes wide and wild now. She was beginning to frighten Sophie.

Oh, it was him. It was definitely him. "It looked like him," Sophie offered in a voice she hoped was nonchalant. Was Valentina so desperate to marry off Sophie to a duke that she would insist Phillip prove his identity? Is that what Lord Hillsdale had told her? If so, they were both mad. But knowing Valentina, she'd come up with that idea on her own.

It was too outlandish to be anyone else's. No doubt she'd been inventing it on the ride home last night.

"This wouldn't be the first time an imposter attempted to snatch a title," Valentina insisted, moving to stand at Papa's arm and read over his shoulder. "A duke's title is nothing to be taken lightly and Hugh will not give it up easily."

Frowning, Sophie glanced at her stepmother from the sides of her eyes. What in the world was *that* supposed to mean?

CHAPTER SEVEN

Acrros Mayfair, in the breakfast room of Clayton's town house that morning, Phillip drank his black coffee and perused the paper. Just as he'd antici-pated, the Society pages hadn't been kind to Sophie. Or him.

Missing Duke Finds His Way Home was one headline. He expelled his breath. Those fools. He'd never been *missing*. He'd been purposely staying away. But what did he expect from London's infamous gossip rags? They'd been even less kind to Sophie, insisting she'd angrily confronted him because his return meant her *fiancé* would no longer be a duke. Unkind at best. Though Phillip knew precisely what one marquess spy would have to say about the rumors.

As if on cue, Clayton's butler entered the room and cleared his throat. "Your Grace, the Marquess of Bellingham is here to see you."

"You don't say," Phillip mumbled under his breath.

The butler's brows drew together in a frown. "Your Grace?"

Phillip raised his voice. "Show him in, please, Humbolt."

The butler turned and left, and moments later Bell and

Clayton came striding into the room. Bell took one look at Phillip and said with an arched brow, "Did you see them?"

Phillip blinked at Bell. "The papers?"

"Yes," Bell replied.

"I did," Phillip said simply.

"Would you care to discuss it?" Bell asked, his hands braced on his hips.

"There's nothing to discuss." Phillip wanted nothing more than for his friend to stop acting as if Sophie's engagement should mean something to him. Leaving her without news all these months had clearly opened the door to her choosing another man, and she'd done so. Phillip would have to live with that for the rest of his life. But it certainly didn't make Sophie guilty of a crime.

"There *is* something to discuss," Bell replied, pressing his lips together. "Grimaldi sent me here with strict instructions to keep you away from Miss Payton. You mustn't spend *any* time in her company."

"Given that the last time I saw her she was nearly running away from me, I doubt that will be a problem from now on," Phillip replied simply, a purposely bland smile on his face.

"Yes. I heard about that from one of our men at the ball," Bell said.

Of course. Bell's men knew everything.

While the two men spoke, Clayton had been busy speaking with the butler, ordering tea for Bell, who never drank alcohol, and ordering brandies for himself and Phillip, despite the hour. Now Clayton turned back to face the other two. "Did your men learn anything at the ball, Bell?"

Bell shook his head. "Unfortunately, no. We were looking for the reactions from a few different men, one of whom was Hugh Grayson, of course, but for some reason, he decided not to attend at the last minute."

"You don't think he got wind that I'd be there?" Phillip asked, rubbing his jaw.

"We don't know for certain," Bell replied, leaning against the back of a nearby chair. "It's a possibility. Your mother didn't tell anyone, did she?"

Phillip frowned. "I doubt it. I asked her not to and made it clear that my safety depended on it. Regardless, she wouldn't have spoken to anyone who knows Hugh. She cannot abide him. Never could."

"She has good reason from what you told me," Clayton interjected, shaking his head.

"What's that?" Bell asked, cupping a hand behind his ear, obviously eager to hear the story.

Phillip shook his head, too. "Mother told me that besides auctioning most of our personal effects from the London town house and the country estate after Malcolm's death, Hugh has been making an ass of himself around town."

"How so?" Bell prompted.

Phillip leaned back in his seat. "Apparently, he's been trumpeting his title to get admission to White's and lording himself about, demanding favors and political alliances and all sorts of things he knows little about."

"Political alliances?" Bell asked, narrowing his eyes. "Such as?"

Clayton sighed. "I heard he asked Lord Blakely and Lord Collins to change their votes on the Employment bill."

"The Employment bill?" Bell echoed. "What does Hugh know about the bloody Employment bill?"

"Precisely," Phillip replied. "According to Mother, he's made a fool of himself all around town. Running up charges at every shop and pretending to know things about Parliament, of which he's sorely ignorant." Phillip turned to Clayton. "I remain in your debt for the things you saved from the auction, Clayton."

After getting wind of Hugh's auction plans, Clayton had come to London and purchased nearly all the items. They were in storage at Clayton Hall, awaiting Phillip's return to his properties. And Clayton hadn't stopped there. He'd gone on to Tattersall's to bid on and win Phillip's famous Arabian horse, Alabaster. The fine horse ended up costing Clayton a small fortune, given that Thea's brother had been bidding on the same horse for *her*. It was how the couple met, actually. Regardless, Phillip owed Clayton a great deal.

"Please don't mention it," Clayton replied. "It's nothing you wouldn't have done for me had I been in your place."

Phillip nodded. It was comforting to have as loyal a friend as Clayton. The man gave Phillip credit for saving his life when they were children and Clayton had been caught under a current in a stream, held down by a branch. But Phillip felt the same, and he *would* have done the same for Clayton had he been in his place.

Bell plucked at his bottom lip. "Curious that the man who came to town to revel in his newfound wealth and status would take an interest in bills in Parliament. That hardly seems like Hugh."

"I agree," Phillip added. "It's quite curious."

Clayton shrugged. "A seat in Parliament conveys great power and Hugh strikes me as the type who is easily seduced by such things."

"You may be right," Bell allowed. He turned back toward Phillip. "If your mother didn't tell Hugh you were back, why do you think he skipped the Cranberrys' ball last night?"

"I've no idea," Phillip replied. "It couldn't be a coincidence, could it?"

Bell cracked a grin. "I don't believe in coincidences."

"How did I know you would say that?" Phillip replied, returning his friend's grin.

"Regardless of his reasons for bowing out last night," Bell

continued, "the less Hugh knows about what you're planning, the better. Now as for the papers—"

Phillip groaned. "Must we discuss the papers?"

The butler returned just then with the drinks and Phillip waited until all three of them had a cup in their hands and had taken a seat before lifting his glass and saying, "To my return to Society!" He even managed to say it in a half-convincing voice, as if he hadn't spent last night in a fevered sweat, fearing the next crowd he would be forced to enter.

"Frankly, it went better than I thought it would," Clayton replied with a laugh, lifting his glass too.

"Some of it," Phillip replied, taking a sip of brandy.

"Which part didn't?" Bell asked, arching a brow.

"I'd rather not discuss it," Phillip said.

"Miss Payton, no doubt. Which brings us back to the papers," Bell warned.

"I know. I know. Spare me. You still believe Sophie had something to do with Malcolm's death." Phillip took a larger swig of brandy than he ought.

"You read it for yourself, didn't you?" Bell reasoned. "The entire *ton* knows her little tantrum was because you are taking away her chance at being a duchess."

Clayton winced.

Phillip took a deep breath. It was time to tell both of his friends the entire truth. "First, there was no tantrum. And second, she and I were nearly engaged to be married once." He eyed Clayton. "I'm surprised Thea didn't tell you."

Clayton contemplated his drink. "Thea said she refused to repeat what she'd overheard in that drawing room, as she was desperately pretending to be a piece of furniture."

Phillip couldn't help his bark of laughter. "That was good of her. But had you been there, you would have heard Sophie ask me if I still planned to offer for her."

"She asked *what?*" Bell choked out, nearly spilling his tea upon his lap. He pushed the cup atop the table in front of him and turned to glare at Phillip. "You're telling me she tried to engage herself to *you* in the past, is now betrothed to *your cousin* who was recently named the duke, and when you reappeared last night seemingly back from the dead, she asked you to offer for her again? By God, the woman has no shame!"

Phillip closed his eyes and took another deep breath. "I understand how it sounds when you put it that way, however, the fact is—"

"Is there *another* way to put it?" Bell demanded.

Phillip scowled. "There's more to the story, Bell."

Bell leaned back in his chair and crossed his arms over his chest. "Oh, really? Do tell."

Phillip opened his mouth to speak, but promptly shut it. How *could* he explain Sophie's actions? He knew the truth (or thought he did), but the best way to prove it was to exonerate her. Not to sit here and have the same blasted argument with Bellingham again and again. And to exonerate Sophie, Phillip needed to find out precisely what had truly happened to his brother. Immediately.

Bell waded into the silence. "Look, it's possible that I'm wrong, but it's also possible that I'm right. Sophia Payton may well have been in on the plot to take the title from you and your brother and possibly had a hand in Malcolm's murder, and until we know more, you need to stay far, far away from her."

Phillip remained silent and took another sip. There was nothing left to say. Bell's pronouncement wasn't surprising, but it also didn't mean that Phillip intended to comply. He had plans of his own for handling the debacle his life had turned into since he'd been pulled from that battlefield half-dead. And since he had no intention of informing Bell of his plans, a subject change was well in order.

"Now that I've revealed myself to Society as being very much alive, we must find Malcolm's killer as soon as possible," he declared to the marquess, focusing the topic on the issue at hand.

"I quite agree." Bell plucked at his lip again, and a sly smile slowly spread across his face. "And to that end, I suggest you invite your cousin over for a nice little family visit."

A similar smile spread across Phillip's face. He'd been greatly looking forward to his confrontation with Hugh. "With pleasure."

CHAPTER EIGHT

Sophie had slipped out of her father's salon earlier and headed toward the back of the house, intent upon hiding in the gardens until Hugh left. The early afternoon air cooled her face, but her insides were still a roiling mass of nerves. How was she supposed to feel about everything that had happened in the last two days? It wasn't as if such things were written in etiquette books or taught by tutors. What precisely was a young lady to do when one's former love, whom one had previously believed to be dead, reappeared suddenly the night after one had become betrothed to his first cousin?

She was glad Phillip's return almost certainly meant an end to her engagement to Hugh. Didn't it? Wasn't that why Valentina had asked Hugh to pay her a visit today? To tell him she and Papa were calling off the engagement. What else might they discuss? But what in heaven's name had Valentina meant when she'd said, "A duke's title is nothing to be taken lightly and Hugh will not give it up easily?"

At the time, Sophie had decided not to respond. She'd hurried from the room, not wanting to hear any more. She'd only antagonize her stepmother if she argued with her. The woman wasn't thinking correctly. She was clearly in such a state her thoughts were addled. As usual, Papa would have to calm Valentina down and make her see reason.

Sophie trailed a bare hand along the top of the hedgerow that followed the garden path. The path lined the area between the park and Papa's house. The house and Sophie's dowry were nearly the only things Papa still had that were worth anything. He'd spent most of his fortune on extravagant gifts to keep Valentina happy. Valentina liked to remind Papa that as the daughter of a viscount, she had lowered herself to marry him. Papa was merely a knight, after all. Which was another thing that bothered Sophie. It never made sense that a duke—the Duke of Harlowe, of all people—would want to marry *her*. Phillip had been nothing more than a second son when they'd fallen in love, and they *had* fallen in love. Phillip hadn't planned to offer for her to fulfill some sort of familial obligation. Theirs was to be a love match. Hugh's offer had never had so much as a hint of love involved. From nearly the moment Hugh had taken over the title, Valentina had waged a campaign so great it had apparently overwhelmed the new duke. He had begun courting Sophie as soon as the Season began. Valentina had wasted no time ensuring an engagement took place and had rushed to get it to the papers.

Of course, Sophie had never thought it right to accept the suit of a man who had taken Phillip's brother's place in Society. But Hugh could have been any man. It didn't matter. She hadn't felt a thing for anyone since she'd heard the news of Phillip's death all those months ago. Her heart had shattered into a thousand pieces, only remaining to keep her body alive. She hadn't even been allowed to grieve for Phillip, for goodness' sake, because she was never his official *fiancée*. The most she'd told Valentina was that she was in love. When her stepmother had asked her what title her betrothed had, she'd replied that he was untitled. She'd never forget the woman's response. "Forget him, immediately." Of course, Sophie hadn't forgotten him. But she'd also never admitted to either Valentina or her father that the man she'd loved had been Phillip Grayson.

Now, Sophie's mind raced with myriad questions. Where had Phillip been all those months? Why hadn't he written her? Why in heaven's name would he allow his cousin to take up the title if he were still alive? None of it made any sense. And Phillip remained cryptic about the answers.

Tears filled her eyes. *Damn him. Damn him. Damn him.*

What was Phillip doing coming back from the dead? And looking like Adonis to boot? She'd spent the last year grieving for him. Praying for death herself. Putting off Valentina every time she tried to coax Sophie out into Society to smile and pretend she wasn't broken. *Damn him again.* What was Phillip doing back here now? Now that she had just walled up that part of her heart and locked it away for good. To keep it as a beautiful but painful memory.

And how could this *possibly* end?

Obviously, she and Phillip would not pick up where they'd left off. She couldn't trust him, and she clearly didn't even know him any longer. Not to mention she did not know how he felt or what he wanted or even why he'd never come forward to say he was alive.

The worst part was, despite everything, she still couldn't help but wonder what Phillip thought. He must believe her to be a capricious opportunist to have turned her attention to his cousin. But each time she had the thought, it was quickly replaced with another one...what did she care what Phillip Grayson thought of her? He was an ass. A man who'd allowed her to think he was dead for nearly *an entire year* and refused to explain himself. She owed him nothing.

Sophie had wandered off the path into the park. She'd made her way not twenty paces along a dusty side road when a carriage came rumbling toward her. Still lost in her thoughts, she barely looked up. The carriage came to a stop not a length in front of her, and as she walked past, the door opened, and two large male arms emerged. She was grabbed and hauled inside, a hand covering her mouth to keep her from screaming.

CHAPTER NINE

Phillip pulled Sophie close against his chest. "It's me," he whispered in her ear. She went from kicking and fighting him with everything she had to going completely still.

"If I take my hand off your mouth, will you promise not to scream?" he asked, trying not to think about how good she smelled or how soft her body was pressed against him.

She nodded woodenly. He removed his hand and let her go. She quickly kicked him in the shin and scrambled to the opposite seat.

"Ouch." He rubbed his shin. "I told you it was me. Why did you kick me?"

Her eyes flashed fire. "I promised not to scream. I never promised not to kick you. The kick was for frightening me nearly witless. What's wrong with you, grabbing unsuspecting ladies out of the park that way?"

Phillip bit his lip. She was ever truthful. He knew he'd been right to doubt Bell. "I'm sorry I frightened you. I could think of no other method to get you in here. Would you like me to open the window?"

Sophie glanced down. She'd always been afraid of enclosed spaces. Carriages were particularly difficult for her. Phillip had remembered.

She jerked her head in a nod. "Yes, please," she said quickly before glaring at him again and demanding, "What is happening? Faking your own death? Abduction? Who are you?"

The coach had already taken off. Phillip had given Clayton's driver orders to trot around the park. He leaned over to open the window next to Sophie to allow in air and light as he said, "I cannot tell you everything now. But I needed to speak with you and can hardly pay you a call."

"You could have pulled up alongside me and *asked* me to come into the carriage," Sophie pointed out, her arms still tightly crossed over her chest.

He arched a brow. "Would you have said yes?"

She lifted her chin. "No."

"Then my approach was correct."

Her arms remained crossed, but the glare fell away from her face. "Fine. Let's discuss something you *can* tell me. You let me think you were dead. What sort of sick bastard would do that?"

Phillip expelled his breath, closed his eyes, and resignedly admitted he couldn't even tell his own mother.

Sophie remained unimpressed. "Couldn't or wouldn't?" she demanded.

"Both."

She pushed forward until she sat on the edge of the seat cushion. She studied his face. "Why? Why didn't you write, Phillip? You owe me an explanation."

Phillip scrubbed a hand through his hair and met her gaze. "There's something I must ask you first."

Her nostrils flared. She was obviously still beyond upset with him. "You realize how ironic it is that you demand answers to *your* questions when you refuse to answer *mine?*"

Phillip met her gaze. "I know. It must be this way. Just know...I regret it. I regret hurting you, Sophie. But I *must* ask you something first."

Sophie shook her head and swallowed. "Fine." She folded her hands in her lap and sat up straight. "What do you want to ask me so badly you had to snatch me out of the park?"

Phillip took a deep breath. He had needed to ask her this in person. He needed to see her face when she replied. He would know if she was telling the truth. And it shouldn't matter to him any longer, but it did. "Why, Sophie? Why did you become engaged to *my cousin* of all people?"

Her head snapped to the side as if she'd been slapped. She kept her face turned away from him, not meeting his eyes. "Does it matter?" Was it his imagination or did her voice shake?

"Perhaps not to you," he replied, searching her profile for any hint of her true feelings.

He saw her swallow a lump in her throat. "You've been gone for years, Phillip. Until yesterday, I thought you were dead."

He scrubbed his hand through his hair again. "But why *Hugh?*"

"I don't even know you anymore," she shot back, turning to meet his eyes again, hers filled with anger. "The man I knew...the man I loved..." Her voice faltered. "He would never have done that to me."

"Why are you refusing to answer my question? You're just either simply being petty or—" *Dear God.* It would cost him everything if she said yes to the next question, but he *had* to know. "Are you...in love with him?" He couldn't keep the incredulity from his voice.

There was a long pause and then, "What does it matter?" Her voice trembled.

"Do. You. Love. Him?" Phillip repeated through clenched teeth.

She lowered her gaze to her lap. "No."

Profound relief washed through him, but the joy was soon replaced by pain when she narrowed her eyes and added. "I'm not in love with *anyone*."

Expelling his breath, Phillip fell back against his seat. Those words hurt more than he wanted them to. But frankly, it was better this way. He could no longer be the man Sophie needed. She deserved better. "Is that so?"

She nodded jerkily, her jaw tight. She looked up, but still didn't meet his eyes. Tears glistened in hers.

"Then why are you engaged to him?" Phillip asked one more time. Why? Why couldn't he let it go?

Her gaze snapped back to Phillip's, and she waved a hand in the air. "You know how these things work, Phillip. Papa and Valentina arranged it. I never told them about..." She glanced away again.

"About what?" Phillip prompted, moving forward in his seat again.

"About us," she whispered, her voice catching.

"That was probably for the best," Phillip murmured.

"Was it? Now the entire city thinks I hate you for taking away my chance at being a duchess." She crossed her arms over her chest and stared out the window.

It was on the tip of Phillip's tongue to ask if that was true, but he just couldn't hurt her like that. He and Sophie knew the truth, and asking her to say it out loud would only be cruel. No. If he knew anything for certain, it was that she loved him...once.

He closed his eyes briefly. "You've answered my questions. Now I'll answer yours."

She leaned forward, watching him carefully, obviously prepared to hear whatever he was willing to share.

"First, I was…ill. I'd been gravely injured on the battlefield. I nearly died."

She sucked in her breath. "I see." She seemed to consider that news for a few moments before she added, "Very well. But it seems to me you could have at least written once you had recovered adequately enough to—"

"I did write, Sophie. I did." He met her gaze directly.

Her eyes widened. "I never received—"

"I wrote you. I told you I was alive." He took a deep breath. "But I never posted the letter."

Sophie's lips rounded into an O. Pain flashed across her features. "So you admit you were *able* to write me?"

Phillip nodded, still searching her face. "I *did* write you."

Her chest was heaving with her obvious indignation. "But you never sent it. *Why?*" she demanded. "I don't understand. Make me understand, Phillip."

He scrubbed a hand through his hair. "It's complicated and there's so much to—"

"Why didn't you send the letter, Phillip?" she asked through clenched teeth. "Why did you allow me to think you were dead all this time?"

Fine. If she wanted the truth. She would get it. "I couldn't tell you the truth because…Malcolm was murdered."

Sophie gasped, and her eyes flew wide. Genuine surprise registered on her face. She'd have to be a consummate actress to be faking that reaction. "No," she breathed, shaking her head, her hand at her throat. "No."

Phillip could hear Bell's voice in his head telling him he'd shouldn't have told her, but this was Sophie. Whatever they were to each other now, they'd been so much more once. She couldn't have changed entirely.

"We aren't entirely certain yet," Phillip continued, "but the

Home Office, my friend Lord Bellingham and his superior officer, Grimaldi, strongly suspect it."

"Murdered?" she repeated, her eyes filled with astonishment and unshed tears. "But why…how?" Confusion was etched on her brow.

Phillip bit his lip and glanced away. "He died after the *ton* already thought I was dead."

"But—"

Phillip kept his gaze pinned to Sophie's pretty face. Bell would never forgive him for this. But Phillip had seen the truth in her eyes. He'd heard it in her voice. She didn't love Hugh. "We think Hugh may be involved."

Sophie's jaw dropped, and she fell back in her seat, blinking wide eyes. "What?" she breathed. She sat in obvious stunned silence for several seconds before raising her gaze to meet Phillip's again. "Oh, my God. Hugh *is* the one who stood to gain the most, isn't he?"

"Yes. We intend to begin our investigation this afternoon. We're starting with him. And…"

"And what?" Sophie prompted, her terrified gaze searching his face.

Phillip lowered his head and blew out a final breath. He'd tortured them both enough. It was time to end this conversation, to get back home…to his reckoning with Hugh. "I must ask you to promise not to tell *anyone* about the suspicions around Hugh. *No one* must know. Do you understand?" He lifted his head once more.

"You have my word." She nodded and stared out the window again, but he could see the tears still shimmering in her eyes. A few moments later, she smoothed a hand over her forehead. "Well, now we're all in a fine mess, aren't we? Apparently, I'm betrothed to a murderer."

Phillip nodded. "Bell and I intend to find out the truth as quickly as possible. Until then, you must act as if you know nothing about this." Phillip met her gaze. "And as for your betrothal, it seems to me the engagement announcement in the paper never actually named your betrothed."

"Don't be ridiculous. Valentina would have ensured it stated that I am betrothed to..." She paused, her eyes widening.

"The Duke of Harlowe," they said in unison.

"Me," Phillip breathed.

CHAPTER TEN

Sophie sneaked back into Papa's house through the servants' door near the back stoop. Phillip had let her out in the same spot in the park where he'd pulled her off the path. No worse for wear, she supposed, though she made him promise the next time he needed to urgently and privately speak to her, he would do the gentlemanly thing and simply ask her into the carriage.

The things Phillip had told her in the coach raced through her mind. Apparently, he had essentially abducted her to ask why she'd become engaged to Hugh. At first, she'd been convinced that it must mean Phillip cared. A little, perhaps. That it bothered him to see her engaged to another man. He'd even had the nerve to ask her if she *loved* Hugh.

When Phillip had first asked, she had swiftly turned away so he couldn't see the hurt and anger that had to be plain on her face. *Of course* she didn't love Hugh. Though she'd certainly never believed him capable of *murder*, of all ghastly things. She still couldn't fully grasp that possibility.

But once Phillip had told her he suspected Hugh of killing his brother, Sophie's hope that Phillip actually cared died a quick death. If she had declared her undying love and loyalty to Hugh, she doubted she would have learned the truth about Malcolm's murder. Sophie swallowed hard. *Dear God.* Had Phillip suspected *her* of knowing about the murder?

Sophie shook her head. How had this all become so complicated? One moment, she'd been heartbroken and resigned to a loveless marriage. The next she'd been furious, seeing Phillip again and dealing with his refusal to tell her why he'd pretended to be dead all this time. Now she didn't know what she wanted, other than for Papa and Valentina to quickly retract her engagement to a possible murderer. She couldn't tell them that, of course. But her social-climbing stepmother would see to it. Valentina couldn't possibly want to keep the engagement to a man who no longer held the title she'd so coveted.

Sophie wouldn't miss Hugh, of course. But that didn't mean she could just fall back into Phillip's arms, either. Even though the news of Malcolm's murder certainly explained why Phillip had been reticent to trust anyone, he should have trusted *her* with the news. Second, he may have told her about Malcolm's murder, but that hardly meant Phillip still wanted her. After all, she might have been good enough for him when he was a second son, but he was a duke now. And even though he may have demanded an explanation for her betrothal to Hugh, that hardly meant he was still in love with her. He'd made no indication of his feelings for her. Even if he hadn't suspected her, he might only be watching out for her safety since he suspected her new *fiancé* was a killer. She'd told him she didn't love anyone. She'd lashed out at him due to anger. The truth was she did not know how she felt any longer.

An image of Phillip on the verandah at the Miltons' ball struck her again. Back then, every time she saw him, her knees went weak. Oh, who was she kidding? Her knees went weak when she saw him now. When he'd whispered in her ear that it was him who had plucked her off the street, she'd nearly relaxed against him and turned to wrap her arms around his neck and ask him to hold her. Which was madness. And when he'd asked her if she'd like him to open the window, it had nearly wrecked her. He'd remembered she was frightened of small spaces.

But what did any of that matter? Over three years separated them now. Too much had happened. Not just his deception and her betrothal to the man who took his title. It felt as if a vast gulf existed between them. Phillip was no longer the honorable young soldier she'd known and fallen in love with, and she was no longer the starry-eyed debutante who'd adored him.

At the end of their discussion, Phillip had said that she was engaged to the Duke of Harlowe. That was him now. He must have been jesting. But it begged the question...now that Hugh was no longer the duke, would the marriage contract even be valid? She needed to speak with her father. Or even better...Papa might still be speaking to Hugh in the study even now. He'd been planning to pay them a visit, hadn't he?

She climbed up the servants' staircase and sneaked down the corridor to stand outside the door to Papa's study. Thank heavens Valentina wasn't there. That lady often liked to linger outside Papa's door to eavesdrop. At least she'd taught her stepdaughter well. Sophie pressed her ear to the door and concentrated.

"Look, Mr. Grayson," Papa was saying. "I assure you. I am not calling off the engagement. We simply need a bit of time to...think things over. See where things stand."

Sophie's brows shot up. What? Why *weren't* they calling off the engagement? Papa was no longer calling Hugh by his title, which indicated that he, at least, has grasped reality.

"You mean you need time to decide how best to call *off* the engagement," came Hugh's angry, petulant voice.

"What do you expect us to do?" came Valentina's voice, high-pitched and filled with worry. Oh, so *that* was why the woman wasn't eavesdropping. She was inside the study with them. "You're no longer the duke. Or won't be, soon enough."

"I wouldn't count on that, my lady," came Hugh's overly confident voice.

Sophie frowned. What precisely did *that* mean? Why were they all acting so oddly about the rules of inheritance? There was no question. The title belonged to Phillip. Sophie's stomach sank, just as it had nearly nine months ago when she'd learned that Malcolm Grayson had died.

"Regardless," came Papa's voice, firm and dismissive. "Until the title issue is worked out, we intend to postpone any decisions about the engagement. We must be clear on the title first."

The sound of a chair being pushed back told Sophie that at least one of them was standing. No doubt Hugh. "This is not over yet, Sir Roger," Hugh declared. "I'm leaving now, but I implore you to give me a few days."

Sophie turned and quickly rushed back down the corridor to the servants' staircase. She didn't stop until she was in her bedchamber with the door closed behind her. She hadn't wanted them to see her skulking about in the hall. She pressed her back against the door and expelled her breath. She'd had quite enough of this. Everyone was acting strangely lately. Phillip was snatching her out of the park, Papa and Valentina were refusing to call off her engagement to a man who was not only no longer a duke, but who might be a murderer. And Hugh, that dolt, was acting as if he still might have some claim to a title that clearly belonged to his cousin. It was madness.

Sophie refused to sit around quietly and allow everyone

else to make important decisions about *her* future. She was in a unique position to help Phillip get the answers he sought. If her own *fiancé* was a killer, she intended to find out.

What had Hugh said again? This is not over yet? Give me a few days? Sophie had a sinking feeling she might know precisely what *that* was supposed to mean. And she needed to warn Phillip.

CHAPTER ELEVEN

As expected, Bell was knocking on Clayton's door before dinner that evening. Phillip strolled casually into the salon to meet with the marquess, with what he hoped was a suitably recalcitrant look on his face.

Bell's arms were tightly crossed over his chest while he glared at Phillip. True to his character, the man wasted no time.

"Why did you do it, Harlowe? You know we're following you day and night...for your own safety."

Of course, Bell was asking about Phillip's meeting with Sophie in the carriage earlier.

Phillip nodded. "Yes, which is how I knew I'd be perfectly safe," Phillip replied. "Besides, I seriously doubted that a debutante out for a walk in the park would harm me in some manner."

"You still haven't answered my question. *Why?*" Bell insisted, his arms still crossed, his glare still firmly in place.

Phillip took a deep breath. "I had to talk to her, Bell. Alone. I had to ask her something."

Bell paced over to the fireplace and expelled his breath. "I understand, but be careful, Harlowe. This *isn't* a game we're playing."

"You don't think I know that?" Phillip ground out. He shook his head. He understood why Bell didn't want him to see Sophie, but he'd had to look into her eyes and know for certain if she loved Hugh. She didn't. Thank God. And Phillip refused to stop and examine precisely why that revelation meant so much to him.

Humbolt knocked on the door to the salon, interrupting Phillip from his thoughts. "The Duke of, *er...*" The butler's face turned the red of a ripe apple. "Mr. Hugh Grayson is here to see you, Your Grace."

Phillip nodded. He had sent Hugh a note earlier indicating that he expected the man to appear at Clayton's doorstep at his first opportunity. It had been a demand, not a request.

Bell snapped his fingers. "Hugh is here. This is perfect. I'll just pop into the next room and listen if you don't mind. Give us five minutes, Humbolt."

"I'm surprised it's taken Hugh this long to show up." Phillip nodded to the butler as approval of the five-minute directive, and Humbolt retreated.

Precisely five minutes later, Phillip was sitting in a winged-back chair facing the fireplace, pretending to be reading a book when the butler returned with Hugh directly on his heels. Phillip barely glanced up, and he purposely didn't stand.

The look on Hugh's face was...disappointment. His cousin was wearing fine clothing the likes of which Phillip had never seen him in. But there was something odd about them. He looked like a boy playing dress up. The clothing was ill fitting if you asked him. "It *is* you," Hugh breathed, his shoulders drooping.

Phillip quirked up the side of his mouth in a half-smile.

"Did you think I was an imposter?" he replied, waving to the chair across from him to offer his cousin a seat.

Hugh lowered himself into the chair, looking like a man defeated. "I couldn't be entirely certain until I saw for myself, of course."

Phillip tipped his head to the side and regarded his cousin. The man was older, for certain. Blond hair receding. A bit more jowly. A few wrinkles on his forehead. But the beadiness of his dark eyes remained. And the same sour expression Phillip remembered from their childhood sat heavily on Hugh's face. Hugh had been the type to cry, throw fits, and blame others. Always arguing and wanting his way. Always insisting nothing was his fault. No doubt about it. This was the same Hugh. "I still have the scar on my leg that you gave me when we were children, if you care to see it," Phillip finally offered, reminding Hugh of the time his cousin had purposely tripped him during a hike through the forest near Graystone Manor. The action had caused Phillip to fall against a large branch that has ripped his breeches and tore a gash in his calf.

Hugh's nostrils flared. "That won't be necessary."

Phillip gave him a tight smile. "Glad to hear it. I suppose you being *pleased* to see me alive was too much to hope for."

Hugh ignored that remark, instead saying, "I suppose you'll be going to Whitehall immediately to handle the matter." There was a hint of apprehension in his voice.

Phillip narrowed his eyes at his cousin. Did the man honestly think he would waste any time restoring his title now that he was back? Phillip clenched his jaw. Hugh had ungodly nerve. He had taken over the title, the households, *and* his would-be *fiancée*, *of course* Phillip would waste no time restoring them. The first two, at least. "If by 'the matter' you mean restoring the title that is rightly mine, then yes. I do intend to handle it. Immediately. I've already sent letters to the Chancellor of Parliament and the Prince."

"Lord Hillsdale handles such matters."

"I've already spoken with Hillsdale, as well," Phillip replied, giving his cousin a tight smile. "In fact, he's due to pay me a visit any time now."

Thwarted anger flashed across Hugh's dull features. "The obvious question is, if you've been alive all these months, why are you just now coming forward?" He nearly barked the question.

Phillip kept a tight smile pinned on his face. "Suffice it to say I wasn't capable of coming forward...until now."

"Where were you?" Hugh demanded. "Someone must have known you were alive. Clayton, perhaps? Why didn't *he* come forward?"

Phillip arched a brow. "May I assume you're *not* pleased to see me alive?" He chuckled humorlessly.

Hugh's only answer was to narrow his eyes on Phillip. He'd always been a hateful boy, and now he was a hateful man. "You do look different. How do I know you're *not* an imposter?"

Phillip took a deep breath. Really? Hugh wanted to play this game. "It's been three years and I've been through quite a lot. War will do that to a man. As for proving myself? You used to have a small doll that you carried around with you everywhere when you were a child. Your father made fun of it mercilessly, as I recall."

Hugh's eyes narrowed to dark slits, and a mixture of rage and hate radiated from them. "I set that doll on fire."

"Yes," Phillip drawled. "One of the many charming things you did as a child. It wasn't the only thing you set on fire, if I recall. Remember the tree house?" Phillip and Malcolm had made it together in a large oak at their grandfather's estate. They'd spent all summer building it and when Hugh had come for a visit after it was complete, a mysterious fire destroyed it later that same day.

Hugh's face turned a mottled purple color. "You cannot prove that I —"

Phillip waved the protest away with his hand and steepled his fingers over his chest. "I have a question for you, and I expect an honest answer."

Hugh blinked slowly. "What?"

Phillip kept his gaze trained on his cousin's face. "Of all the ladies in the *ton*, why did you engage yourself to Miss Payton?"

Hugh shrugged. "Lord Vining introduced her to me. He said she was the catch of the Season. Only the best for the Duke of Harlowe. Not to mention she's beautiful."

"Hmm. Lord Vining, eh?" Phillip narrowed his eyes.

"That's right," Hugh insisted.

Phillip rubbed his chin. He'd asked his cousin the question to gauge whether Hugh was aware of what Sophie meant to him. Based on his casual reply and the lack of a gleam in his eye, Phillip had his answer. Hugh didn't know that Phillip had once been in love with Sophie. But it begged the question...what did Lord Vining know about it? If anything? It was far from true that Sophie was the catch of the Season. Why would Vining tell Hugh that?

"You've always wanted what you couldn't have, Hugh. This time, you took my brother's title and my *fiancée*. I won't allow you to take anything else."

"Your *fiancée*?" Hugh's eyes widened. "What are you talking about?"

Phillip stared at his cousin through the narrow slits his eyes had become. "Before I left, I was nearly betrothed to Miss Payton. Are you saying you didn't know that?"

"I didn't!" Hugh moved forward in his chair and tugged

on his cravat, an earnest look on his face. He actually looked a bit…frightened.

Phillip believed him. Hugh had always been a rubbish liar. The look on his face told Phillip that no matter Hugh's crimes, becoming betrothed to Sophie hadn't been meant to hurt Phillip. But there was one more question he had to ask before he sent this fool on his way. "Do you love her?" He couldn't help himself. He had to see the truth on his cousin's face.

Hugh sat back in his chair and crossed his arms over his chest, frowning. "What sort of nonsense—?"

"Do you love her?" Phillip repeated in a booming voice that brooked no disobedience.

Hugh rolled his eyes. "Certainly not. I barely know the girl."

Phillip arched a brow. He had his answer. Hugh clearly didn't give two whits about Sophie. He'd only wanted her because someone else had instructed him to. That sounded *exactly* like his cousin. Quite believable. Now to the final details. "I expect you to relinquish all Harlowe properties to me, of course."

Hugh straightened his shoulders. "I'll begin removing my things from the town house."

"Good. I expect you to be out by week's end," Phillip drawled.

"Week's end!" Hugh's face turned purple again. "That's not nearly enough time. You must be reasonable. We can discuss this like adults."

"Week's end," Phillip repeated in that same voice that brooked no further discussion. "And I want the ledgers for all the properties and all expenses on my desk here no later than tomorrow morning. Send your man along with them. I intend to take a full account of everything you've bought and sold."

Hugh kept his gaze pinned to the floor. He tugged nervously at his cravat. "There was an auction—"

"Yes, I'm well aware. An auction *you* instigated," Phillip drawled.

"How was I to know that you—?"

Phillip put up a hand. "Enough. Now, I expect you and all of *your* belongings, anything not purchased with Harlowe monies, to be out of *my* properties by week's end."

"But…my new things," Hugh blustered. "You cannot mean—"

"Leave anything purchased with my money. If I cannot return them, I'll hold an auction of my own." Phillip gave his cousin a pleasant smile.

Fuming, Hugh stood and smashed his hat back on his head. "You've always hated me," he barked. "I was merely protecting our family name and you'll see me ruined for it. You're mad!"

"Perhaps," Phillip replied calmly, inclining his head toward his cousin, "but I'm back. And we'll do things *my* way from now on. By the by, you should know that my priority is ensuring my brother's death is fully investigated."

Hugh froze and turned slowly to eye Phillip. "What? Malcolm died of an attack of the heart."

"So they say," Phillip clipped.

Hugh narrowed his eyes at Phillip. "What is that supposed to mean? Dr. Brigham said so himself," he insisted.

Phillip kept the smile pinned to his face. "Take it however you'd like."

Eyes blazing dark fire, Hugh turned and stalked from the room. He'd only been gone a few moments before Bell and Clayton pushed open the door from the adjoining salon and stepped inside.

"That was well done of you," Clayton commended.

"It was also quite interesting, I thought," Bell replied. "That bit about Vining."

"I thought so, too," Phillip replied, bracing an elbow on the arm of his chair.

"Tell me. Does your family have any past connection with Lord Vining? Any reason for him to dislike you?" Bell asked Phillip.

"Not that I'm aware," Phillip replied. "But I suppose it's possible he and Malcolm had a falling out."

"Hear anything about that in Parliament, Clayton?" Bell asked the viscount.

Clayton pursed his lips and rubbed his chin. "Hmm. Nothing comes to mind. Vining isn't much of an authority in Parliament. He's more of a toady for the Tories. Same lot as Sir Reginald Francis. He's always seemed to be something of a clod to me."

"Sir Reginald? That blowhard?" Bell replied, rolling his eyes.

"One and the same," Clayton replied. "Tell me, Harlowe. Did your cousin seem guilty to you? After speaking with him, do you believe he had a role to play in Malcolm's death?"

Phillip shook his head. "I honestly couldn't tell in the few minutes of our conversation. He did seem surprised when I mentioned I'd be investigating Malcolm's death. That was unexpected."

"That could have been out of fear as much as surprise, if he was involved," Bell pointed out.

A sharp rap on the salon door was immediately followed by Humbolt stepping inside. He was holding a silver salver with a folded piece of vellum on it. "My apologies for the interruption, my lords," the butler said, "but I was told to get this message in the hands of the duke as quickly as possible.

It's from Sir Roger Payton's household." He hurried over and offered the missive to Phillip.

Phillip stood and pulled the paper off the salver. He quickly broke the seal with his finger, unfolded it, and scanned its brief contents. Once he'd read it, he dismissed Humbolt, and turned to his friends.

"It's from Sophie," Phillip announced. "It says, 'Hugh was just here and refused to admit he no longer holds the title. He told my father and Valentina it wasn't over yet and asked them to give him a few days. I believe you may be in imminent danger.'"

CHAPTER TWELVE

Sophie shouldn't have come to the Covingtons' ball tonight. She'd told Valentina she didn't care if everyone was gossiping about her engagement, but once they'd entered the room, the loudness of the whispers behind hands and fans became a near cacophony. Every step she took involved eyes following her and each time she glanced at anyone, they quickly diverted their gaze. It was tedious. If balls were a location where one could find the ridiculous, tonight *she* was the object of ridicule.

Sophie wore a light blue gown with a sarsenet underskirt and the pearl earrings and necklace her mother left her. Two of the few pieces of jewelry she'd been able to keep from Valentina's grasp.

Sophie wished someone—anyone—would have the temerity to come up to her directly and ask if she still considered herself engaged to the Duke of Harlowe now that Hugh was likely to lose the title. She would commend them for their audacity, at least. Everyone else was avoiding her as if she carried plague.

After Hugh had left this afternoon, Sophie had been summoned to Papa's study, where her father and Valentina had sat Sophie down and told her they were 'considering their options' when it came to her engagement. They didn't want to make a hasty decision, they explained. *Whatever that meant.* Sophie had been flabbergasted. Why in heaven's name wouldn't they choose to call off the betrothal immediately? She did not know, and she didn't dare ask. She didn't care for the ambitious gleam in Valentina's eyes. Instead, Sophie had retreated to her bedchamber, where she'd quickly fired off the missive to Phillip (delivered by one of Papa's footmen) to warn him that something seemed amiss. She'd no idea how Phillip had reacted, but she hoped he'd keep himself safe.

Now, Sophie was standing in the Covingtons' ballroom drinking a lukewarm glass of lemonade, wondering precisely how long she would have to stay to keep the gossips from saying she'd run away, when a tall shadow appeared at her side.

She looked up to see Phillip standing there. He was wearing fine black evening attire with a startling white shirt front and cravat tied expertly at his neck. A silver and white waistcoat and perfectly shined black boots completed his ensemble. He looked like a god descended from the heavens, and the spicy, soapy mixture of his scent made her legs wobble.

"Would you care to dance?" he asked in his most charming voice. The voice she'd held onto in her memories all these years.

Sophie blinked at him. For a moment she could almost pretend that time had stopped, and it was three years ago, and none of this awfulness had happened. They were in love and were about to share a dance at a ball, just as they had in the past. Only this time was different. And Phillip probably shouldn't even be here tonight. His life might well be in danger.

"Do you think that wise?" she finally managed to reply, hoping her voice sounded as nonchalant as his.

Phillip cracked a smile. "Since when has wisdom been a requirement for dancing? If that's the case, half the floor should be cleared."

Sophie smiled despite herself. The man had a point. She'd been hoping someone would be bold enough to speak with her. She simply hadn't expected it would be Phillip, of all people. Besides, she was curious about what he would say to her while they danced. Hadn't they said everything that needed saying?

"The gossips will have conniptions if we dance," Sophie pointed out.

Phillip shrugged. "They're already at their wits' ends. Might as well give them something even more interesting to jabber about."

His smile was infectious and when he offered his black-clad arm, Sophie wrapped her long, white-gloved one around it. Feeling the warmth from his body sent a shiver through her. She hoped he didn't feel it. He escorted her onto the dance floor and took her into his arms as a waltz began to play.

"I'm sorry for the gossip at your expense," he said, smiling down at her.

Sophie lifted her chin and looked up at him. "You really must stop apologizing, Your Grace." It felt odd to call him Your Grace. But then again, it had always felt odd to call Hugh by the honorific, too.

"It seems that's all I've done since I've returned," Phillip replied. "Apologize."

"Yes, well. No more," she replied before deciding it was time to change the subject. "Why did you ask me to dance?"

A smile reappeared on Phillip's face, and it made her

insides tumble. "Ah, that is simple," he said. "Because I *wanted* to dance with you."

She tamped down the pleasure his response made her feel. "You know it'll only make the gossip about us worse."

"I know," Phillip replied, "but I've spent many years of my life doing what was expected of me rather than what I wanted to do, and I've decided I'm through with that."

Sophie's smile expanded. "That sounds wonderful, actually."

"Doesn't it?" he replied, before leaning down and asking in a conspiratorial whisper, "You know what would make the gossip even worse still?"

"What?" she asked in a similar whisper, realizing that for the first time in months—since the news of Phillip's supposed death—she was truly enjoying herself…and smiling.

Phillip's grin turned positively mischievous. "If I escort you outside for some fresh air."

She sucked in her breath and lifted her brows, but the smiled remained on her face. In fact, it turned a bit wicked. "We'd send half the ballroom into an apoplectic fit," she said gleefully.

"Yes. Won't it be fun?" Phillip replied with an unrepentant grin. "Someone quite wise once told me that most of the fun of attending a ball is either the ridiculousness to be found or the possibility of a scandal, and I've sorely missed ridiculousness these last few years."

"Very well," Sophie replied, positively warming to the idea, "if they're going to gossip, let's give them something worthwhile as fodder."

They stopped dancing and Phillip offered his arm once more. She took it, and with heads held high, they both marched off the dance floor toward the French doors at the back of the room and out onto the verandah.

A cool breeze swept across Sophie's face as soon as the door shut behind him. She pulled in a deep breath. She felt as if she'd just escaped Bedlam. The verandah was empty, and the space smelled like jasmine and newly shorn grass. Sophie dropped her arm from Phillip's and spun in a circle, suddenly feeling as if she were a carefree eighteen-year-old debutante again and Phillip was her beau.

She swiveled to face Phillip, her ice-blue skirts skimming along her stockinged ankles. "Oh, that *was* fun!"

"It was, wasn't it?" Phillip replied with a laugh. She took Phillip's arm again, and they strolled together toward the balustrade at the far end of the porch to look out at the darkened gardens.

"I can only guess how many of them will press their noses against the windows to watch," Sophie added, tossing back her head and laughing. It was also the first time she'd truly laughed in an age.

Phillip glanced back toward the windows behind them. "Don't worry. None of them will dare come out here."

"I hope not. It feels so good to be free of their stares, if only for a few moments," Sophie replied, reluctantly pulling her arm from his and placing her hands on the cool stone balustrade to keep them occupied.

"I agree," Phillip replied.

"That was daring of you," she continued, watching him from the corners of her eyes. "The Phillip I used to know wouldn't court such scandal."

Phillip leaned down, his forearms braced against the balustrade. He stared off into the darkened gardens behind the house. "The Phillip you used to know hadn't faced death," he said quietly.

Sophie sucked in a breath and nodded slowly. "Of course." She bit her lip and ventured on the topic she hadn't dared mention until now. "How badly were you injured…in battle?"

She stared expectantly at the side of his face, hoping the story wasn't too awful for him to recall.

He remained silent for several moments before saying, "Quite badly. I survived, but..." He bowed his head and stared at the stone beneath his boots.

"But what?" she prompted, not wanting to cause him painful memories but desperately wanting more detail about the time he'd been gone.

"The truth is..." He lifted his head and met her gaze. Pain shone in his green eyes. "I was going to say...not for the Frenchmen's lack of trying."

Sophie turned and looked at him. She could tell that he'd wanted to say something else and had obviously thought better of it. She couldn't help herself. She reached out and laid a hand on his sleeve. "What happened, Phillip?"

He leaned down and bowed his head. Then he took a deep breath. "I was shot off my horse. Left to die on the battlefield."

"No!" Sophie breathed, shaking her head.

"I was found two days later by a pair of soldiers scouring the field for anything of value."

Sophie gasped and her hand flew to her neck. "That's hideous."

"That's war," he replied soberly. "I was only fortunate it was English soldiers who found me. Not the French. Or I'd have been run through with a bayonet. I had to keep silent until I could see their uniforms and knew they were ours."

Sophie took a deep breath and tried to banish that awful thought from her mind before asking quietly, "What happened to you...after they found you?"

Phillip straightened up and lifted his gaze toward the dark treetops. "The ball went all the way through my right shoulder."

Sophie swallowed and shook her head. Her throat ached.

"After I fell," Phillip continued, "I had broken ribs, blood loss. Then there was the lack of water. Later, the infection nearly killed me. I was sick for…"

"Months," Sophie finished for him, clutching at his sleeve. She knew it had been months because he'd been gone that long. She reveled in the feel of his pulse beneath her fingers, knowing that he was truly standing here next to her, alive and well. This wasn't a dream. "I'm sorry, Phillip. Sorry that happened to you, but I'm not sorry you're back now."

He didn't look at her, just continued to stare silently out at the night.

Sophie swallowed hard. The ache in her chest spread to her throat. The way he'd said the words, the quiet pain in his voice. Until this moment, she hadn't truly considered how bad off he might have really been. She'd only been angry that he had returned, looking fit as a fiddle without having ever written to let her know he was alive. It had been selfish and short-sighted of her.

"I should have died out there," Phillip finally said. "I was broken."

"No," she said quietly, but forcefully. "Don't say that. Please never say that." And then, to change the subject a bit, she said, "Where did you recover? Spain?" Her voice was too high and sounded far too bright, as if she was asking him about a holiday instead of a crisis that nearly took his life.

"No. Once they knew I was alive, Lord Bellingham came for me. Seems the son of a duke gets special treatment, regardless of whether he wants it."

"Where did you go?" she asked, frowning.

"Clayton's estate…in Devon."

"That's where you were all these months?" she breathed. It all made sense now. No wonder Phillip seemed so close to both Lord and Lady Clayton.

Phillip nodded.

"If it's any consolation," Sophie said, desperately trying to lighten the mood, "the papers claimed you died a hero."

The hint of a smile tugged at his lips, but his expression remained blank. "There is nothing heroic about war."

She nodded, swallowing the enormous lump that had formed in her throat. "I'm sorry I was so angry with you...at the Cranberrys' ball," she finally murmured.

"You had every reason to be angry."

"But I didn't know—"

"I didn't tell you what happened to me so that you would feel sorry for me, Sophie. I told you because..."

"Because?" She lifted her gaze to his. "Why? I thought about it, Phillip. Malcolm died two months after the battle. Did it take you the entire last year to recover?"

Phillip's jaw went tight. "It doesn't matter."

Sophie frowned. "What do you mean? Of course it matters."

He paced away from her. Then turned to face her, a determined look in his eye. "The fact is that I'm no longer the man I used to be. The war...changed me. You may not want Hugh, but you shouldn't want me, either. I would no longer make a good husband for you, Sophie."

The tears that had been burning the backs of her eyes since they'd began this discussion came rolling down her cheeks.

"Don't cry, Sophie," he said. His face turning tender, he stepped toward her and pulled a handkerchief from the inside pocket of his coat. He wiped her tears away with the soft linen and handed it to her.

"You don't want me any longer, Phillip?" She hated herself for asking the question. It sounded so needy.

"I will always want you, Sophie," he whispered, lifting a hand and tracing her cheekbone. He pushed an errant curl behind her ear. Then he leaned down, pulled her into his arms, and kissed her.

The first shock of his lips on hers made Sophie freeze, but as his mouth moved against hers, hot and searching, she opened her lips and allowed him inside. She lifted on tiptoes, wrapped her arms around his neck, and moaned against his mouth, leaning fully into his kiss. Never wanting it to stop. Oh, God. She'd dreamed of this so many times, lying alone in her bed at night. This was what she'd wanted for so long. To be back in Phillip's arms.

Phillip splayed a hand against her lower back and pulled her tight against his body. She moaned again. His mouth slanted across hers, and he gently cupped one of her cheeks as his tongue continued its gentle assault. Finally, he shuddered and pulled himself away from her, taking a step back as if to solidify the distance between them.

He expelled his breath. "Do I need to apologize for that, too?" he asked, eyeing her carefully.

"Of course not," she breathed. "But I don't understand. First, you told me I shouldn't want you, then you told me you *do* want *me*. What am I to think?"

"I am sorry," he said. "I had to kiss you...one last time."

His words were like a dagger to her heart. She might not be entirely certain of what she wanted, but hearing Phillip tell her it was over was more painful than she ever could have guessed. She had to try one more time to get him to tell her the truth.

"What happened to you on the Continent, Phillip? Why do you think I shouldn't want you?"

"You've always been too good for me, Sophie," he replied, touching her lightly under the chin with his forefinger.

They both knew that had been an evasive reply. Fine. He was clearly refusing to tell her what she wanted to know. Well, she refused to cry any more. She'd cried quite enough over Phillip Grayson. Wiping her tears and returning his handkerchief to him, she took another step back. She'd agreed to come out here half to antagonize the gossipmongers and half to remind him he might be in danger. But this encounter had taken an awfully painful turn. She could bear no more. Not tonight. Her heart was too fragile.

Instead, she mentally shook herself and forced herself to change the subject. "Why did you risk coming here tonight? Didn't you get my message? You may be in danger."

His smile held an edge of irony. "I've been in danger since the moment I stepped back into town. But I saw Hugh this afternoon, and he led me to believe he may attempt to claim that I'm an imposter."

Sophie frowned. "An imposter? That's ludicrous. How can he possibly think that claim would work?"

"I'm not certain he thinks it any longer after meeting with me, but I suspect he had hoped I was an imposter when he spoke to your father and stepmother earlier."

Sophie shook her head. Accusing Phillip of being an imposter was absurd, of course, but it would explain what Hugh had meant when he'd asked Papa and Valentina to give him a few more days. Perhaps that's why they had been willing to wait. Did they honestly believe Phillip was an imposter as well? If so, they would all be sorely disappointed.

Phillip offered his arm again. "Allow me to take you back inside before the gossipmongers die from fits of agony. I wouldn't want to be responsible for Lady Cranberry's demise."

"Agreed. If that happened, who would we have to judge for wearing far too many feathers in her hair?" Sophie replied, allowing a brief smile to flit across her face.

She took Phillip's arm and allowed him to lead her back toward the ballroom. One thing was certain: Phillip was still hiding something, something he didn't want her to know about the time he was away. If Sophie would ever learn the truth, it wouldn't be from Phillip. She would have to go to someone else.

And she knew just who that might be.

CHAPTER THIRTEEN

Ater a restless sleep plagued by more nightmares, Phillip had spent the entire morning in Clayton's study going over the ledgers that a harried-looking solicitor had brought over first thing. From what Phillip had determined so far, Hugh had wasted no time spending the Harlowe fortune. Phillip wasn't surprised. His cousin had always been a spendthrift. But was he a murderer? The question haunted him.

Bell was on his way over to fetch Phillip for their meeting with the doctor. Yesterday, Hugh had mentioned Dr. Brigham, the doctor who'd declared Malcolm's death an attack of the heart. But there was another doctor. Dr. Landry had examined Malcolm's body *before* Dr. Brigham and had later gone to the Home Office to share his concerns that Malcolm had not died of a natural cause. Dr. Landry's suspicions had caused Grimaldi and Bell to become involved and begin an investigation. Phillip hoped meeting with Landry would finally provide some answers he sought.

And as for answers, he had side-stepped providing one to Sophie last night when she'd asked him why he believed she shouldn't want him any longer. The truth was, he hadn't only been physically sick. He'd been mentally sick, too. Not just the nightmares and the sweating, but he'd been so ill he hadn't spoken for months. That's why he hadn't returned to Society sooner, long after his physical wounds had healed. What if that happened to him again? What sort of future could he offer her, being married to a man who couldn't sleep through the night without waking in terror, and who might lose his ability to *speak*, of all things? No. He would rather Sophie hate him than pity him. He couldn't stand to see pity in her eyes. Not to mention the fact that if he told her everything he'd been through, he'd have to give voice to the awful thought that had been lurking in the back of his mind since Malcolm's death...if Phillip had been mentally strong enough to return, to speak, to let everyone know he was alive, Malcolm might still be here. The thought haunted Phillip day and night.

He'd kissed Sophie last night. He couldn't help himself. She looked so pretty and vulnerable and, for a moment, he'd wanted to feel as if the last three years had never happened. He'd wanted to pretend they were who they used to be to each other. He'd told her the truth. He *would* no longer make a good husband for her. She deserved a whole man. A man's whose mind hadn't been shattered by war. A man who could sleep with her wrapped tightly in his arms at night, make love to her, and fall asleep without the specter of a nightmare glowering on his shoulder.

He probably shouldn't have kissed her. She was right when she pointed out that he was confusing the matter. But he hadn't been able to stop himself. His body was a traitor to him where Sophie was concerned. He'd taken her into his arms and wanted to bury himself inside of her. She still wanted him, too. At least there was that. The moan she'd emitted had been proof enough. She hadn't been pretending when she'd responded so passionately to his kiss. That much was certain. Nothing else was.

This morning's papers had been just as unkind as the day before. Apparently, by the time the evening ended last night, the entire Covingtons' ballroom was agog with the gossip that the returning Duke of Harlowe just might have set his sights on Miss Sophia Payton, who was of late betrothed to his *cousin*. Was the new duke planning to take over his cousin's entire existence? Apparently, turnabout was fair play. Phillip shook his head. How ridiculous. And slightly maddening.

Of course, it had been noted that Phillip and Sophie had been seen waltzing and then leaving the dance floor together. Phillip could only imagine Bell's reaction. The marquess wouldn't be pleased when he heard Phillip had escorted Sophie out onto the verandah last night in front of half the *ton*. And Phillip would find out Bell's reaction soon enough. The marquess was on his way.

Not a quarter hour later, Bell arrived on Clayton's doorstep. Phillip, wearing his hat and coat, opened the front door himself. The marquess had his hands firmly planted on his hips while he gave Phillip yet another condemning look.

"I know what you intend to say, so I'll spare you the need to say it," Phillip said, tipping his hat and giving Bell a jaunty smile.

Bell shook his head and turned back down the steps to return to his carriage, with Phillip behind him. "You'd think a man whose life I was trying to save would be more thankful." He gestured for Phillip to enter the coach ahead of him.

Phillip pulled himself up into the conveyance and threw

himself into the jade-green velvet seat facing forward. "I do appreciate it, Bell. Believe me."

"Yet you continue to spend time alone with Miss Payton," Bell replied with a sigh, taking the opposite seat.

"I suppose you won't care if I tell you I hardly thought she was hiding a pistol or some poison in her reticule at the ball last night."

"This isn't a jest, Harlowe," Bell replied, frowning. "Your brother was killed in his own home. Last night on the verandah, anyone could have happened by. That ballroom and the surrounding grounds were filled with people. If you had been harmed, we wouldn't have been able to track down the culprit easily."

"Sophie sent me a note warning me I might be in danger yesterday, yet you still think she may have had something to do with Malcolm's death?" Phillip asked.

Bell gave him a skeptical glance. "If she did have something to do with it, she may have sent you that note to throw you off her path, convince you to trust her."

"I do trust her, Bell," Phillip replied softly.

Bell rolled his eyes. "You're a fool in love. But you don't have to be convinced. I am convinced for you."

Phillip narrowed his eyes at his friend. "But you have no proof."

"Not yet. But I have my suspicions, not to mention the word of Malcolm's valet, who said he saw an unknown young woman leaving the house just before he found Malcolm's body."

"Correct me if I'm wrong, but the valet didn't see the woman's face, did he?" Phillip prodded.

"No, he didn't," Bell replied. "But Miss Payton is hardly helping her case for innocence by betrothing herself to your cousin, confronting you upon arrival, and now spending time with you alone. In a word, it looks...bad, Harlowe."

"Those things don't prove she was at Malcolm's house that night," Phillip pointed out.

"I agree," Bell replied. "They *don't* prove it was her. Let's go speak to Dr. Landry. Perhaps he can provide more details."

~

THE BETTER PART of an hour later, Phillip and Bell were settled in chairs in Dr. Landry's sitting room, while a maid served them tea. The doctor was a middle-aged man with white-streaked dark hair and a full mustache. He had bright blue eyes and a sharp nose, and he wasted no time coming directly to the point.

"I wondered when you'd come," Dr. Landry said after they'd each been poured a cup and the maid had retreated from the room.

Phillip's brow shot up. "Really?"

"Yes. It's been several months since I spoke with General Grimaldi, but I always believed he took my concerns seriously."

"Quite seriously," Bell replied, lifting his teacup to his lips. "Please begin with what you know about Malcolm Grayson's injuries."

The doctor took a deep breath. "By the time I saw him, he'd been brought here to my offices in the back of a carriage. The constable was with the body."

"Go on," Phillip prodded.

"I had the opportunity to examine him for the better part of two hours before Lord Vining arrived," Dr. Landry continued.

Phillip frowned and glanced at Bell. "Lord *Vining?*"

"Yes." Dr. Landry nodded. "He said he was sent to investigate."

"Investigate what?" Bell asked, narrowing his eyes. "At that point, was there anything to investigate?"

"At first I didn't think so," Dr. Landry continued, "but by the time Lord Vining arrived, I'd changed my mind."

"Why?" Phillip asked, setting down his cup and leaning forward in his chair.

The doctor nodded. "I told Lord Vining I found what I believed was a stab wound near your brother's heart. Though it had been delivered to his back."

Phillip sucked in his breath. "Stab wound?"

"Yes," Dr. Landry continued. "Admittedly, it was small and quite difficult to locate. If I hadn't looked so carefully and for so long, I might well have missed it. I suspect it was caused by a small dagger, but I have no proof."

"But if there was a stab wound, there must have been blood," Bell pointed out, frowning.

"That's just it," Dr. Landry replied, shifting his gaze from Bell to Phillip. "There wasn't any blood. If the duke was stabbed, someone cleaned up the blood before his body was brought to me."

Phillip leaned back into his chair and expelled his breath. "What?"

Dr. Landry nodded. "I also found that odd."

"What did Lord Vining say when you told him your suspicions?" Bell asked.

"He said because of the duke's title and what I'd found, they would need to get a special doctor to examine the body, one who worked with Parliament for important cases such as this. That's when Dr. Brigham was consulted."

"I see," Bell replied, exchanging a glance with Phillip. "And did you ever speak to Dr. Brigham yourself?"

"No," Dr. Landry replied. "But I wrote down all of my findings and I gave them to Lord Vining with instructions to make certain Dr. Brigham was given the information along with the body."

"Did you ever hear anything else from Lord Vining?" Phillip asked.

Dr. Landry shook his head. "No, Your Grace. In fact, I never heard another word about it from anyone. The next thing I knew, the papers indicated the duke had died of a condition of the heart and your cousin was coming from the countryside to assume the title."

"And that's when you went to the Home Office?" Bell prompted.

Dr. Landry glanced back and forth between them both. "I must admit, I thought about it for some time. Several weeks, in fact. It was early in the morning when they brought me the body and I began to doubt whether I'd truly seen what I thought I'd seen. If they gave my note to Dr. Brigham and he didn't agree, perhaps I'd been wrong."

"Did you ever suspect they did not give him the note?" Phillip asked.

Dr. Landry shrugged. "I had to wonder. In the end, I decided the best thing to do would be to tell someone at the Home Office. If they investigated and found nothing, well, at least I'd done what I could."

"We truly appreciate your coming forward," Bell replied.

"Yes," Phillip agreed. "If it's determined that foul play was involved in my brother's death, my family owes you a great debt of gratitude."

Dr. Landry waved his hands in the air. "No need to thank me, Your Grace. I did what anyone in my position should have done. I'm only sorry I waited."

"And I'm sorry you had to wait even longer for this visit," Bell replied. "But Harlowe here has been unwell, and he insisted he be with me to investigate."

Bell and Phillip stood.

"I understand, my lords," the doctor said, rising from his chair as well. "I'm only glad to have been of service."

Bell nodded again. "If you think of anything else, doctor, please don't hesitate to contact me." He pulled a calling card from his inside coat pocket and handed it to Dr. Landry. Then he and Phillip turned toward the door to leave.

"There is one other thing I didn't mention," Dr. Landry said.

Both Phillip and Bell stopped and turned back to face him.

"Would you like the name of the first doctor who examined the body?" Dr. Landry asked.

Phillip and Bell exchanged a stunned look.

Phillip arched a brow. "*First* doctor?"

CHAPTER FOURTEEN

Lady Clayton came floating into the blue salon at the front of her town house and smiled prettily at Sophie. "Good afternoon, Miss Payton. A pleasure to see you."

Sophie swallowed and lifted her chin. "Thank you for taking my call, Lady Clayton."

"Please call me Thea."

"Very well…Thea," Sophie replied, nervously tugging at her gloves. Why did she suddenly feel so out of place? She'd decided to pay Lady Clayton a visit this afternoon to see if the viscountess could provide any additional information on Phillip's circumstances while he'd been recuperating at her country estate. But now that Sophie was here, sitting in the fine lady's drawing room, she felt like a fool for having come. Lady Clayton—no, *Thea*—had seemed quite kind and reasonable the night of the Cranberrys' ball when she'd escorted Sophie down to the drawing room to meet Phillip, but that hardly meant she was willing to tell Sophie secrets about her friend.

Both ladies took their seats, and Sophie cleared her

throat. She might as well get this over with. "I cannot stay long. My stepmother will be looking for me," she began.

Thea's brow furrowed. "You didn't tell her where you were going?"

Sophie concentrated on sipping the tea that she had been served. She didn't meet Thea's gaze. "I try not to tell her much. We do not get along well."

Thea's brows shot up. "I hate to hear that, Miss Payton."

"It's quite all right. I've learned to live with it."

Thea opened her mouth as if she was about to speak, but she shut it again before finally saying, "I suspect your visit has something to do with Phillip."

"Erm, yes, it does have to do with...His Grace," Sophie managed, feeling slightly envious of the fact that Thea got to call him Phillip.

"I thought so," Thea replied, still smiling.

Sophie took a deep breath. At least she hadn't been tossed out on her ear, yet. She might as well proceed. "The truth is... I've come to ask you a question."

Lady Clayton eyed her with clever, inquisitive gray eyes. "What's that?"

Sophie took a deep breath. Now that the moment was at hand, she squirmed in her seat. She scratched her cheek. But she finally forced herself to out with it. "Why didn't His Grace, er, Phillip, come back to London? After he was well enough to, I mean?" Once the words were out, Sophie bit her lip and plucked nervously at her peach-colored skirts. The question seemed to hang in the air like an awkward cloud of smoke.

Lady Clayton blinked and looked away briefly, while Sophie's forehead began to sweat. It was stifling in the drawing room. She plucked at the neckline of her gown.

"He was recuperating," Thea finally offered, the hint of a

smile on her lips as if what she'd just said was a complete explanation.

"Yes," Sophie replied quickly. "He said as much, but when I last spoke to him, it seemed to me there was something about his recovery that he didn't want to share with me. He said…" Sophie decided to tell the whole truth. It might make the viscountess more willing to share. "He said he would no longer make me a good husband."

Thea glanced away, looking as if she was contemplating whether to answer the question or run from the room to escape. "Miss Payton, I think your question is best asked of Phillip," she finally replied softly.

Sophie kept a steady gaze trained on the viscountess. She'd come this far. She wasn't about to back down now. "But Phillip won't tell me. I was hoping you might."

Thea turned back again and searched Sophie's face, before setting down her teacup and pressing her hands to her knees. "Miss Payton, will you allow me to be frank?"

"Please do," Sophie replied, folding her hands in her lap in a similar fashion and mentally preparing for the worst. Nothing good ever came after the words "allow me to be frank."

"I have a good feeling about you, and I'm usually a fine judge of character," Thea continued.

Sophie narrowed her eyes. "Thank you…I think."

"You seem like a nice young lady, and I know Phillip cared deeply for you."

Pain slashed through Sophie's chest. Thea had used the past tense. Sophie nodded woodenly, swallowing the lump in her throat. "Go on," she finally prompted.

"But Phillip is my dear friend. And you…you must understand…are betrothed to his cousin."

Sophie straightened in her chair, her head ringing as if she'd been slapped. Was that it? Lady Clayton didn't trust her because she was betrothed to Hugh? Did she dare even attempt to explain herself to his woman? "You don't trust me?" she ventured.

Lady Clayton eyed her carefully. "I see no reason not to be completely honest with you on the subject, Miss Payton. I don't intend to be rude, but the truth is that I'm not certain if I *can* entirely trust you. Lord Bellingham has been quite clear with Phillip that you have been consorting with Hugh for some time now and recently became betrothed to him."

"Lady Clayton, I—" Sophie was just about to attempt to explain to the viscountess that her stepmother had arranged the entire thing when an awful thought flashed through her mind. If his friends didn't trust her, did that mean Phillip didn't either?

"Does Phillip believe *I* had something to do with his brother's murder?" Sophie finally said, her heartbeat quickening and nausea roiling in her middle.

Lady Clayton's eyes narrowed sharply. "How did you know his brother was murdered?"

Sophie briefly shut her eyes and took a deep breath. Apparently, she was only making herself look worse. "Phillip told me. You can ask him yourself. But he never told me he *suspected* me."

Lady Clayton's mouth snapped shut. "I didn't say that. That is a question for Phillip, not me."

Sophie lifted her chin. "But you, your husband, and Lord Bellingham suspect me, and you're Phillip's closest friends?"

Lady Clayton brought her cup to her lips once more and took a sip before saying, "We don't yet know the truth. But whatever it is, we are on *Phillip's* side. We only want the best for him."

As answers went, it was particularly vague, but Sophie read the intent behind every word. That's right. They didn't trust her, and if *they* didn't trust her, it stood to reason that Phillip had his doubts as well.

Sophie stood and faced the door, her jaw clenched, her face a mask of stone. "Thank you for your time today, Lady Clayton. I must get back."

"Miss Payton?" came Thea's voice.

Sophie froze. "Yes," she replied, still facing the door, wanting nothing more than to leave the room immediately.

"At the risk of overstepping my bounds, I must say that I've found in life that one teaches others how to treat them."

Sophie fought the urge to roll her eyes. What was the woman saying now? What did that have to do with Phillip? "What do you mean?" she managed to ask, her jaw tight.

Thea's certain voice sounded from behind. "Only that accepting poor treatment from others—your stepmother, for instance—leads to *more* poor treatment. It's a lesson I learned a bit too late in life, I'm afraid."

Sophie's nostrils flared. How dare this woman lecture her on treatment when she'd just been nothing but rude? She whirled to face her. "So, you won't be offended if I reject *your* poor treatment of me today?"

"I'd expect nothing less from you, Miss Payton," Lady Clayton said, while Sophie forced herself to turn again and calmly exit the salon.

The moment she was seated back inside her father's coach, Sophie expelled a deep breath and closed her eyes. Well, *that* had been excruciating. Beyond excruciating. She regretted the moment she'd ever considered paying Lady Clayton a visit. She couldn't blame the woman for her loyalty to her good friend, but she also couldn't shake the notion that Phillip might very well believe *she* was somehow involved in his brother's death. Was that why Phillip had told her Malcolm had been murdered? To see her reaction?

Anger curdled in Sophie's middle like day-old milk.

Phillip had been testing her. His friends didn't trust her. No doubt he didn't, either. Powerful determination rose in her breast. She would help find Malcolm's killer and clear her own name. Then Phillip would know the truth and his friends would realize they'd been wrong about her. And Sophie could walk away from the whole doubting lot of them.

CHAPTER FIFTEEN

Bell was precisely on time the next morning when he came to fetch Phillip for yet another visit to a doctor. Only this time they were going to visit a Dr. Kilgore in Belgravia. Phillip had spent a quiet night last night going over more of the books. He'd discovered just how much his cousin had been spending all over town in the name of the Duke of Harlowe, and Phillip suspected there was even more. That blighter, Hugh, couldn't get out of his town house fast enough. At least Phillip hadn't gone to a ball last night or seen Sophie. He wouldn't have to endure Bell's glare and folded arms this morning. He was through discussing Sophie with Bell.

Thankfully, the moment the coach door shut behind them, Bell got directly to the matter at hand. "What do you reckon Dr. Kilgore knows?"

"I'm not certain," Phillip replied. "But I can't stop thinking about how odd it was that Lord Vining arrived at Dr. Landry's house the night of Malcolm's murder, saying he was investigating. You know I met Vining at the Cranberrys' ball."

"And?"

"And he was a sweaty little man who seemed quite preoccupied with my return."

"I agree. It's odd that Vining was there that night. What did he have to do with it?" Bell replied.

"Nothing, according to Clayton." Phillip settled back against the seat. "Apparently, Lord Vining has little to do with succession laws and nothing to do with death investigations of noblemen."

Bell nodded. "I'd say we should pay Vining a visit next, but if he did have something to do with it, I don't want to alert him to the fact that we're investigating."

"It's probably too late for that. I told Hugh I was planning to investigate Malcolm's death," Phillip said. "If he's allied with Vining, Vining probably already knows."

"Yes, but Hugh may believe you're simply planning to speak with Dr. Brigham, who would tell us precisely what he told everyone else…that Malcolm died of a heart condition."

"Good point. Let's see what Kilgore has to say," Phillip replied as the coach pulled to a stop in front of the doctor's house.

The two men alighted and jogged up the stairs to the front door. After a few moments, a sleepy-looking butler opened the door and allowed them in. Not a quarter hour later, they were sitting in the doctor's study with the man himself. He was older than Landry, with a full head of white hair and a round face that looked pallid and rough as if it had been scrubbed too thoroughly.

"Lord Bellingham, Your Grace, how may I be of service?" Dr. Kilgore asked.

"Thank you for seeing us, doctor. We were hoping you'd be kind enough to answer some questions about the day my brother died," Phillip began.

Fear flashed across the doctor's face just before he

glanced away. "I'm not certain what help I can be, Your Grace." His eyes darted around the room.

"We understand you were the first to examine Malcolm's body," Phillip continued, exchanging a glance with Bell.

The doctor shook his head. "No, no. I—"

"Think carefully before you continue," Phillip warned. "I don't want to make a liar out of you."

The doctor cleared his throat and tugged at his cravat. "Well, I—"

"We already know you saw Malcolm's body," Bell pointed out. "We need you to tell the truth."

Dr. Kilgore bowed his head and expelled his breath. "Very well. What do you want to know?"

"What happened that night?" Phillip asked, narrowing his eyes at the doctor. "Were you called directly to Malcolm's town house?"

"Yes," the doctor replied, sighing. "It was quite early in the morning. My butler woke me. He told me I was needed at the duke's residence immediately."

"When you got there, what did you see?" Bell prodded.

"I was escorted to the upstairs corridor. Just outside His Grace's bedchamber. He... His Grace was lying on the floor just outside the door."

"Was he on his back or belly?" Phillip asked.

"He was lying on his back," Dr. Kilgore continued.

"Was there blood?" Phillip asked.

Dr. Kilgore nodded slowly. "Yes, quite a lot. It had pooled on the floorboards beneath him."

"And what did you determine to be the reason for his death?" Bell prodded, watching the doctor's face carefully.

"The valet assisted me in turning him over," Dr. Kilgore continued. "I found what appeared to be a stab wound on his back. Near his heart."

Phillip cursed under his breath. "So you never believed

his death was caused by a condition of the heart?" Phillip prodded, studying the doctor's face for any hint of deception.

Dr. Kilgore shook his head. "It's true. I never thought your brother died of a heart condition."

"But you refused to say that publicly?" Bell pointed out. "Even after it was reported in the papers?"

Dr. Kilgore shifted uneasily in his seat. "I never had a chance to say anything. After I indicated my findings, Lord Vining told me my services would no longer be necessary."

"Lord Vining was there?" Phillip asked, exchanging another glance with Bell.

"Yes," Dr. Kilgore continued. "He arrived soon after I did. He dismissed the servants and asked me what I believed had happened."

"And you told him you thought Malcolm had been stabbed?" Phillip narrowed his eyes at the doctor.

"Yes," Dr. Kilgore replied.

"But you never stepped forward to tell anyone the truth?" Phillip prodded.

"I... I..." The doctor hung his head. "I'm ashamed to say Lord Vining paid me quite a large sum of money." He tugged at his cravat. "*And* he threatened me."

Bell's head jerked up. "Threatened you? What did he say?"

Dr. Kilgore cleared his throat. "He told me I'd better be careful and think twice before I spoke to anyone about the duke's death. He mentioned my children by name."

Bell nodded. "I understand, doctor."

"But you spoke to Dr. Landry eventually?" Phillip pointed out, still frowning.

Dr. Kilgore nodded. "Only because I heard him talking about it at the club. Landry's a good man. I was worried about him. I didn't want him to get hurt. I took him aside and *privately* indicated that he might want to stop speaking about the duke's death so publicly."

"You didn't wonder if he ever told anyone else? The Home Office perhaps?" Bell asked, a brow arched.

Dr. Kilgore sighed. "Only every single day since then. I haven't been able to sleep for months."

"I hope it goes without saying, doctor, that you should not mention our visit or our discussion here to anyone. Least of all, Lord Vining," Bell continued.

Dr. Kilgore nodded. "Believe me. I don't want any trouble. That's why I've kept it a secret all these months. You have my word."

"I want you to think carefully before you answer this last question, doctor," Phillip said, studying the older man's face.

Dr. Kilgore gulped and nodded.

"Is there anything else you saw that night? Anything at all you think might be of significance?" Phillip asked.

The doctor tugged at his cravat again. "There *was* one other thing I saw that I'll never forget."

Phillip leaned forward, eager to hear the man's answer. "What's that?"

"Forgive me, Your Grace, but there was blood on your brother's back and beneath his body."

Phillip nodded. Nothing more than he'd expected, given the fact that Malcolm had apparently been stabbed. "And?" Phillip prompted.

"And when we moved the body, there was a long, dark hair stuck in the blood. I had no doubt it belonged to a woman."

CHAPTER SIXTEEN

When Sophie arrived back home from Lady Clayton's house, she stood in the foyer plucking off her hat, gloves, and pelisse. She'd been nothing but fortunate that Phillip hadn't been there when she'd paid her call. Lady Clayton's treatment of her still rankled, but now that she'd had more time to think on it, how could she blame the woman? The only thing Lady Clayton knew about Sophie was that Phillip had 'cared' for her and now she was engaged to his murderous cousin who'd taken over the title after his brother's untimely, probably unnatural, death. It looked bad. There was no question about it.

No. Sophie didn't blame Lady Clayton, but she would certainly blame Phillip if he suspected her of being involved with his brother's murder. Sophie intended to confront him on the subject the first chance she got. Did he truly believe she was capable of such an atrocity? If so, he'd apparently never known her at all.

At the moment, Sophie intended to confront Valentina and ask her why exactly she refused to call off the engagement. It made little sense. Hugh was clearly hiding something from all of them. And there was no doubt. Phillip was *not* an imposter. The entire notion that he could be was preposterous.

"Have you seen my stepmother?" she asked Roberts, the butler, after handing him her coat and bonnet.

"My lady is in the rose salon." The man gave her a sneer. Valentina had hired Roberts. In fact, she'd wasted no time sacking the long-term butler Mama had hired in order to install her own man at the front of the house. Sophie had never liked nor trusted Roberts. He clearly did Valentina's bidding. "She has a visitor and has asked not to be interrupted," Roberts continued.

Sophie narrowed her eyes at the butler. Visitor? What visitor? Was it Hugh? "Thank you," she replied simply, knowing Roberts would not be inclined to tell her more. Instead, she made her way up the staircase, intent on convincing Roberts she was merely retiring to her bedchamber.

Five minutes later, she was back, peering down the staircase. Roberts was nowhere to be seen. He was probably smoking on the back stoop with Valentina's hateful lady's maid. Sophie hurried down the stairs, across the foyer, and down the corridor to the rose salon.

The double doors were closed, and she glanced each way to ensure none of the servants or Papa were coming, before plastering her ear against the door. Who was Valentina in there talking to?

"I told you, Valentina. I'll take care of it," a man's voice said.

Sophie sucked in her breath. Take care of what? The voice was familiar, but she couldn't quite place it. It definitely wasn't Hugh, however.

"When? This has already got out of hand," came Valentina's tart reply.

"I'm weighing the options," the man's voice replied.

"Which are?" Valentina snapped.

"These things must be handled delicately...with finesse," the man continued.

"What do you plan to do?" Valentina's voice took on a nasally, whining sound. It was the same voice she used when she attempted to wheedle more jewelry out of Papa.

"I don't know yet," the unknown man's voice replied, "but I suspect the newest Duke of Harlowe is about to meet with an untimely accident."

A gasp escaped Sophie's throat before she promptly clapped a hand over her mouth. She'd heard all she needed to and didn't dare linger and be seen. She lifted her skirts and hurried back through the corridor and up to her room, all the while trying to place the man's voice. *Think. Think.*

She pushed open the door to her bedchamber and let it shut heavily behind her, rushing over to the window to look down on the street. She would watch when the man left to see who he was. She hovered at the windowsill for what felt like a quarter of an hour before the front door opened and a man descended the steps. He was dressed in the clothing of a nobleman, that much was certain. But his dark cloak and hat blocked any view of his hair or face. *Blast.* And the tree in front of her window obscured her view of the man's carriage. *Blast. Blast. Blast.*

She hurried back downstairs, intent on getting a glimpse of the carriage at least, but she ran straight into Roberts standing at attention at the front door, having obviously just ushered out Valentina's guest. There was no help for it. She had to ask the awful man.

"Who was that leaving just now?" she ventured, trying to

seem as if she hadn't just rushed down the stairs to stare out after him.

"I doubt milady would appreciate her servants gossiping about her visitors," Roberts responded, his eyes narrowed.

Sophie had to struggle to keep from rolling her eyes. "I'm only curious," she offered in what she hoped was a nonchalant voice. She strained to look past the butler in an attempt to glimpse the coach, but Roberts had the audacity to move to block her view.

"I don't think it's any of your business," Roberts replied, glancing outside, probably to ensure the coach had left, before turning on his heel and marching off toward the back of the house.

Sophie watched him go with her jaw set tight. Roberts had been egregiously unhelpful. There was no help for it. All she could do was try to remember whose voice she'd heard. Perhaps she'd recall if she thought about it longer. She quickly discarded the notion of asking any of the other servants. Valentina had hired all of them.

Sophie turned on her heel and slowly climbed back up the stairs to her bedchamber. Whoever the visitor had been, one thing was certain: what he'd said hadn't been some idle threat. He'd threatened Phillip directly. She might be unhappy with Phillip at the moment, but she had to let him know. It wasn't Hugh. Someone *else* was after him.

CHAPTER SEVENTEEN

On the ride home from Dr. Kilgore's house, Phillip turned to Bell. "If there was blood beneath Malcolm's body that night, why have the servants never come forward to indicate foul play? They had to guess it wasn't a condition of the heart."

Bell cursed under his breath. "I never specifically asked Malcolm's valet if there had been blood. I asked him what he'd seen, and he said essentially what Dr. Kilgore told us. That Malcolm had been lying face-up near the doorway to his bedchamber. It's more than possible that they just assumed later that a condition of the heart involved blood loss."

"The valet didn't mention Lord Vining?" Phillip prompted.

"No." Bell shook his head. "The valet said he called the constable. And when the constable arrived, he and the other servants were ordered belowstairs to keep out of the way."

Phillip nodded. "Lord Vining must have arrived after that. But how did he even know about it? Did you ever speak with the constable?"

Bell plucked at his bottom lip. "Yes. And he indicated he escorted Malcolm's body to the doctor. At the time, I assumed he meant Dr. Brigham. It wasn't until Dr. Landry came forward that we knew there had been another doctor."

"Let alone *two* others," Phillip replied, shaking his head.

Bell's coach pulled to a stop in front of Clayton's town house and Phillip alighted.

"Stay inside. Stay safe," Bell warned. "I'm going to speak to Grimaldi...tell him what we've learned. Tomorrow we'll go looking for Malcolm's valet. I have several more questions for the man now that I know what Dr. Kilgore saw."

"Does the valet no longer work for Hugh?" Phillip asked, frowning.

"No." Bell shook his head. "Hugh dismissed most of the servants after he arrived in town."

"Damn him." Phillip jumped from the carriage and tipped his hat to Bell. "Until tomorrow, then."

Bell glared at him. "Stay inside. Don't go out. Now that we know Malcolm *was* stabbed, you are in danger, too."

"I hear you," Phillip replied evenly.

"But are you listening?" Bell prompted, giving him a stern stare.

Instead of answering, Phillip turned toward the house, while Bell's coach took off down the street. Phillip jogged up the stairs to the front door, taking them two at a time. Lost in his thoughts, he opened the door, gave his cloak, hat, and gloves to Humbolt, and strode toward Clayton's study. The room was empty, thank heavens. The last thing Phillip felt like doing at the moment was repeating the entire interview with Dr. Kilgore to Clayton. There would be plenty of time for that later.

Phillip took a seat in the large leather chair behind the desk and leaned back. He stared at the wall and rubbed his chin. The most interesting bit of information they'd discovered so far was Lord Vining's involvement the night Malcolm died. What precisely did Vining have to do with Malcolm's death? Obviously, the man had been involved somehow. Bell had even asked Dr. Kilgore if he was certain the man hadn't already been in the house when he'd arrived.

"I saw the coach with Lord Vining in it pull up myself," Kilgore had replied. "I was looking out the upstairs window." The doctor had gone on to insist that the only other people who had seen the body (other than the killer) were the valet and one of the upstairs maids. Had one of Malcolm's servants killed him? If so, what purpose would that serve? Apparently, it had cost them their positions. Was there another reason? And if the servants *weren't* involved and Lord Vining was somehow, where did the long, dark hair come from? Of course Phillip had also asked Dr. Kilgore if the maid had long, dark hair.

"I remember distinctly, Your Grace," Dr. Kilgore had replied. "Because after seeing the hair beneath the duke, I suspected the maid. She had on a cap, and I purposely asked her to remove it."

"And?" Phillip had prodded, waiting on tenterhooks for the man's answer.

"Her hair was as blond as an angel's, Your Grace," Dr. Kilgore had replied.

"Did you ask the valet if he knew of any dark-haired women who had been, er, visiting?" Bell had prompted.

"Yes, my lord," Dr. Kilgore had replied. "The valet specifically told me he'd seen a dark-haired woman wearing a bright green cape going down the back staircase just before he found the duke's body."

"Yet he didn't follow her? Didn't recognize her?" Phillip had nearly raised his voice and had squeezed the arm of the chair he'd been sitting in until his knuckles turned white.

"The valet told me he was used to being discreet in such

matters," Dr. Kilgore had replied. "And when he first saw her, the valet had no reason to believe anything untoward had happened. By the time he found the duke's body and ran back down the stairs looking for the woman, she had disappeared into the night."

Bell had essentially told Phillip the same thing on their ride back to Clayton's. When Bell had spoken to the valet, the story was much the same. Only he hadn't mentioned the *blood*.

Phillip cursed again and flipped a letter opener over and over in his hand. They had to be missing something. Who was the dark-haired woman? His brother had mentioned no one to him, but Malcolm was hardly in the habit of discussing his light o'loves in his letters to Phillip. Malcolm had mostly written about the estate and Mother. Of course, Bell had decided the long, dark hair was just another item on the list that made Sophie an obvious suspect. But just because the mysterious woman had dark hair didn't prove she had been Sophie. Lots of women had long, dark hair. Phillip agreed with Bell that it stood to reason that the dark-haired woman, whoever she was, had murdered Malcolm, then left and possibly alerted Lord Vining. Either that or the valet or the maid was lying. Had the constable alerted Lord Vining for some reason? Why? Phillip made a mental note to tell Bell they needed to talk to the constable again. He also made a mental note to ask Sophie if she was acquainted with Lord Vining. That might just prove her innocent.

Damn it. Phillip was no closer to knowing what happened to his brother than he had been months ago, but one thing was certain, the first two doctors to have seen Malcolm's body that night agreed...he had been stabbed in the back. Had Malcolm even seen his murderer? Even known who she was? Phillip inwardly shuddered at the notion.

A knock at the door interrupted Phillip from his

disturbing thoughts. He turned to see Clayton's butler standing there. "Yes, Humbolt?"

"A letter has arrived for you, Your Grace," Humbolt said.

Phillip stood and crossed over the thick rug to meet the servant. He pulled the letter from atop the silver salver that the man carried. "Thank you, Humbolt."

The man retreated from the room.

Phillip took the letter back to the desk and opened it. His eyes scanned the page. The note was from Sophie. He quickly read the words she had written.

P,

There's something important I must tell you. Meet me in the park again tonight at midnight. Same spot.

S

A memory of reading Sophie's letters in the light from a lantern while lying on a cold cot in a tent flashed through Phillip's mind. They had always addressed and signed their letters with their initials.

But this was unlike any of the letters Sophie had written him while he'd been on the Continent. This was a warning, but without detail.

The counsel from Bell flashed through Phillip's mind. *Stay home. Stay inside. You are in danger.* Phillip was no fool. Going out at night to meet Sophie might be a terrible idea indeed. He roughly scratched the back of his head. He could ignore the note. He could throw it away and not meet her. But even as he had the thought, he knew he would not do that. Deep in his gut, he knew he *could* trust her. The only question was…could he trust his gut any longer?

Phillip crumpled the letter in his hands. He couldn't tell Bell, or the man would put him under guard or worse, lock and key. No. Phillip would meet Sophie alone.

CHAPTER EIGHTEEN

Sophie paced back and forth in the darkened park. It was unseasonably cold, and she pulled her cape closer over her shoulders to keep from shivering. Beneath it, she was wearing only a simple light green cotton gown with a high-waist and cap sleeves. She wished she'd worn something warmer.

Was she mad to have asked Phillip to meet her so late, in such a secluded place? He might not even come. Her note had been vague. What if he suspected her of being involved in Malcolm's murder, after all? He might think he was walking into a trap.

And if he came, what exactly would she tell him? That some unidentified man had threatened him? What exactly did the man's words prove at any rate? Phillip already knew he was in danger. This may have been a huge mistake.

A crackle in the bushes next to her made her freeze. A hare ran out of a nearby hedge, making Sophie's heart pound. After her breathing slowed back to rights, she laughed instead. "Look at me, frightened of a hare." She shook her head and continued pacing.

Nearly a quarter hour passed, and she was beginning to think Phillip wasn't coming when the soft sound of leaves crunching behind her caught her attention. She turned to see Phillip step out from behind the hedgerow. He looked so handsome wearing all black, this time including a cloak and hat.

"Phillip," she breathed. "You came?" The outline of his face was cast in shadows, but the unmistakable gleam was there in his green eyes.

"I'll always come when you ask," he replied, stepping forward. His eyes scanned the area as if he wondered if they were alone.

Sophie's heart twisted at his words. "Are you all right?" she asked, looking around, too. Who would know she was here? Until this moment, she hadn't even considered the fact that someone may have followed her.

"I hope so," he replied vaguely. "What did you have to tell me so urgently?"

Sophie swallowed. Now that he was standing in front of her asking for an explanation, the whole thing sounded ludicrous in her head. No doubt he'd laugh at her and leave posthaste. She wouldn't blame him. But she also couldn't help but believe that he must trust her after all if he'd come here alone in the middle of the night to meet her.

"I...I overheard something. Something I thought you should know," she offered in a rush.

"Who said it?" Phillip asked, stepping toward her, narrowing his eyes.

"I don't know." She shook her head. Her voice was nearly a whisper.

"What?" The look he gave her was probing.

She tugged at her cape. "I know it sounds odd, and I can't explain it well, but my stepmother had a visitor today and I heard the man say you would meet with an unfortunate accident."

"Who was the visitor?" Phillip prompted, urgency in his voice this time.

Sophie bit her lip. "I don't know."

His looked turned doubtful.

Sophie hurried to explain. "I was listening at the door. I never saw his face," she continued, still biting her lip.

"Did you ask your stepmother who her visitor was?"

Oh, lovely. It sounded even more insane now that he was asking questions. "You'd have to know Valentina. She's been acting so…odd lately. I do know one thing. It wasn't Hugh's voice. I'm certain of it. Someone else is after you, Phillip. A nobleman, by speech and clothing."

Phillip's eyes remained narrowed. "Sophie, do you know Lord Vining?"

Sophie stopped and blinked. "Of course. Papa has known him forever."

The eye-narrowing intensified. "Could his have been the voice you heard this afternoon?" Phillip prompted.

She scrunched up her nose and narrowed her own eyes, trying her best to recall Lord Vining's voice. "Possibly. I haven't spoken to him in quite some time. I recognized the voice, however. I know I've heard it before."

"But you can't be certain it *wasn't* Lord Vining?" Phillip prodded.

"No, I can't." She shook her head.

"You said your stepmother has been acting odd. How so?"

Beneath her cape, Sophie wrapped her arms around herself. "She refuses to call off my engagement. She said she and Papa are still 'discussing it.'"

"Could it be that she actually *wants* you to marry Hugh?" Phillip asked, his brow furrowed.

"I can't see how. Valentina's plan for years now has been

for me to marry the man with the best title possible. Now that Hugh is no longer a duke, it makes no sense that she wouldn't call it off immediately."

He stepped forward and gave her an obvious once-over. "Is that a cape you're wearing? What color is it?"

Sophie frowned and glanced down at the cape. "It's…it's green." Why did the color of her cape matter?

Phillip's scrutiny intensified. He met her gaze. "Sophie, have you ever been to my brother's house? Before his death, I mean."

Sophie sucked in her breath. Her nostrils flared. Was he honestly asking questions that might implicate her in Malcolm's death? Cold anger covered her heart. "I'm certain Lady Clayton told you I paid her a visit. She explained how your friends have suspected me all along. I never thought *you* would believe I would be capable of such a thing, Phillip." She turned away, unwanted tears burning the backs of her eyes.

Phillip cursed under his breath and paced away from her. "Damn it. Thea had no right to tell you that."

Sophie shivered, and her voice betrayed her anger. "Well, she did, and she indicated that my engagement to Hugh points to my guilt."

Phillip stepped around to face her and cupped her shoulders, looking her in the eye. "Look, Sophie, the truth is that Bell *has* suspected you. Besides your betrothal to Hugh, we recently learned a long, dark hair—a woman's hair—was found beneath Malcolm's body the night he died."

Sophie gasped. "What?"

"Yes, and a dark-haired woman wearing a long, *green* cape was seen leaving the house just before his body was found."

"What?" Sophie slowly looked down at the cape she was wearing. "Surely, you don't believe—"

"I don't. But my friends are uncertain, and I cannot clear

your name until we find out who is responsible for Malcolm's death and who is making the threats against me now."

Anger and hurt clashed in her chest. "Believe me. I want nothing more than to learn who the killer is, too. That way, I can tell your friends to go to hell and you and I can be done with each other once and for all."

"Fine." He dropped his hands from her shoulders, and his face became a mask of stone. But had it been her imagination or had pain flashed in his eyes for just a moment? When he addressed her next, there was flint in his gaze. "Then we're agreed that we must work together to learn the truth. Think, Sophie. Whose voice did you hear today?"

Sophie opened her mouth to speak, but her remark quickly turned into a scream.

CHAPTER NINETEEN

Sophie woke slowly to a jostling motion. Her head was pounding, and her stays were cutting into her sides. She felt as if she might retch. She blinked open her eyes and looked around. She couldn't see much. It was still night. She appeared to be lying on her back on the seat of a coach. A fine coach, but an older one, if the smell was any indication. Definitely not a hackney, but not one belonging to anyone of the Quality who had money in their pocket.

Panic shot through her chest. She struggled to sit up, realizing that her wrists and ankles were bound. The skin beneath the thick ropes was chafed and sore. It took several moments to maneuver herself into a sitting position in the dark coach. What had happened?

Oh, God. She'd met Phillip in the park behind Papa's house when two men had come out of the bushes behind him and hit him over the head with something. Then one man had grabbed her and tossed her over his shoulder. They had thrown her in the back of this coach. The pounding in her skull reminded her that once she was inside the coach, she'd been hit over the head as well. Probably because she'd tried to fight the man who'd tossed her inside. She lifted her bound hands toward her head and was able to poke around enough to find a sore spot on top. Curse it. Who had done this?

Desperately trying not to panic in the small space, she used her feet to feel around the coach as best she could. Finally, her slippers encountered something large…and definitely human. An 'oof' sounded from whoever she'd accidentally kicked.

Several seconds passed, and she heard a deep groan. *Please let it be Phillip*, she prayed.

"Who's there?" came his familiar voice moments later. "Sophie?"

She breathed a sigh of relief. "Yes, Phillip, it's me."

"Where are we?" His voice was hoarse.

"We're in a coach going…somewhere. Are you tied up?"

"Yes. Are you all right? I wish I could get the window open for you."

Oh, no. He couldn't make her cry. She might suffocate in here. "I'm all right," she answered, trying to sound brave.

"Who took us, Sophie? The last thing I remember is you screaming. What happened?"

She quickly recounted the facts that she'd recalled. "I must have been followed, Phillip. I'm sorry."

"No, it's my fault. Bell warned me not to go out. I knew I was in danger. Luckily, the Home Office has been following me. It's a good bet they're on our trail."

Sophie breathed a sigh of relief. "Oh, thank heavens."

"Did you see either man? Recognize them?" Phillip asked.

"No. I've never seen either of them before. One was huge, tall and wide. The other was much smaller, but both looked unkempt, like they hadn't washed in several days, and their clothing was cheap and torn."

"Damn it. Hired lackeys, no doubt."

"Have you heard anything? Any indication of where they're taking us?"

"Nothing," Sophie replied, still trying to pull at her wrist ties, even though her skin was raw and bleeding. "I just woke up a few moments ago."

"If they hurt you, I will kill them," Phillip said evenly, but with a determination in his voice that frightened Sophie.

"My wrists are sore, that's all." She took a deep breath. "What should we do?"

"There's nothing much to do until we see where they're taking us. Try to get some sleep, Sophie."

Sophie nodded and closed her eyes. But sleep would never come.

CHAPTER TWENTY

P hillip stayed silent for the remainder of their journey. He was listening for any sound that might give him a clue where they were going. He was specifically hoping their two captors would speak.

He would never forgive himself if Sophie was hurt because of any of this. Whoever the men were, they were clearly after him. She shouldn't even be here. And he would be the one to blame. He'd told Sophie earlier that Bell's cohorts from the Home Office might be following them, but the truth was he knew they were not. And he knew it because he'd purposely eluded them last night.

He hadn't wanted to spend another day answering Bell's pestering questions, so he'd evaded the men in a coach that looked like an innocuous hackney soon after he'd left Clayton's house to meet Sophie last night. No one was coming to help them. But he hadn't wanted to frighten Sophie any more than she clearly already was.

He fought against his ropes for the hundredth time. No use. Someone who knew what they were about had bound him. At least another half hour passed, as dawn broke, before they stopped among some trees along the roadside. A big, beefy man—who was missing an alarming number of teeth—opened the door and blindfolded them.

Phillip tried to remember every detail about him. Beefy blindfolded Sophie first while Phillip watched. "If you harm so much as a hair on her head, you *will* live to regret it," Phillip calmly informed the man.

"Settle down, guv'na," Beefy replied. "Ain't nobody 'urtin' nobody…yet." He guffawed after delivering his speech, revealing more of his poor dental habits.

Sophie kicked and cursed Beefy and even managed to land a decent blow to his shin as he applied her blindfold.

Phillip spent the time while his blindfold was being applied asking a multitude of questions, none of which Mr. Beef answered.

Once the blindfolds were in place, Beefy slammed the coach door shut and they were off again within a matter of minutes. The blindfolds told Phillip they must be close to their destination. Because the sun had barely risen, Phillip estimated that they'd probably been traveling for somewhere between four or six hours, but because he'd been unconscious for part of the journey, he had no way of knowing how often or how long they'd stopped, if at all.

When the horses finally pulled to a stop not a quarter hour later, Phillip heard the coach door being wrenched open. A breeze blew in across his face.

"Come on, ye blighter," said the man he guessed was Beefy as he grabbed Phillip and pulled him bodily from the coach. The man was truly a giant.

"Ye, too, Missy," the giant said.

"Where are we?" Sophie asked in a high-pitched voice that sounded so frightened it made Phillip's heart wrench.

"Keep yer trap shut," Beefy demanded. "Or I'll stuff me old stockin' in it."

Beefy and the other man laughed at that pronouncement.

The threat was enough to keep both Phillip and Sophie quiet as the two men pushed them along in front of them, still blindfolded. The occasional grunt or squeak from Sophie told Phillip she was directly beside him.

There was no use asking more questions, even if they hadn't been threatened with Beefy's stocking. The man clearly had been given orders not to say a word.

After several minutes' walk over gravel, Beefy ordered, "Up these stairs now."

Phillip carefully made his way up a small flight of stairs. A door was opened, and he was pushed inside a building, Sophie still making the occasional noise beside him. They walked through what sounded like wooden hallways for several more minutes before another door creaked open.

"Down them stairs," Beefy ordered.

The musty smell of a cellar hit Phillip's nostrils. He made his way cautiously down the steps. "Be careful," he warned Sophie in a whisper. The steps were rickety. He ensured his body was in front of hers and he would break her fall if she were to trip.

"No talkin', ye!" came Beefy's voice from in front of them. The second man was breathing heavily behind them, nudging them down the stairs with some sort of club.

Once they descended, Phillip heard a flint being struck and just as one captor ripped the blindfold off Phillip's face, a lantern sprung to light.

Blinking against the light, Phillip quickly glanced around, taking in the large room. Barrels and wine bottles lined the closest wall. Bags of flour and wheat were stacked nearly to the ceiling along the opposite wall, and wooden crates, ostensibly also filled with foodstuffs, lined the wall behind them near the staircase. The far end of the space was cast entirely in deep shadows.

Phillip turned to look at his captors. He could finally size up the other man who had traveled with them. The second man was shorter than Phillip and much smaller than Beefy, though he had nearly as questionable teeth. Sophie was right. Both men looked as if they could use a good bath. There was no way these men were the ones who'd wanted Malcolm dead. They were definitely hired lackeys.

The smaller man was busily pulling off Sophie's blindfold. When it was gone, she gave him a narrowed-eyed stare and ire flashed in her eyes.

"I'm gonna remove yer ties, me lady," Beefy said next. "On order o' me master. But don't be trying nuthin'. I've belted a lady afore and won't think nuthin' o' doin' it again."

Sophie narrowed her eyes on Beefy even further. "Charming," she replied in a scathing tone.

Beefy pulled a huge knife from somewhere in his voluminous breeches and sawed at Sophie's wrist ties for a few moments before the ties fell away. Sophie sighed and rubbed her wrists, which were red and had obviously been bleeding. Phillip would see these two blackguards rotting in gaol for what they'd done to her.

The smaller man set the lantern he'd been holding at the bottom of the stairs, before saying, "Ye've got a cot, and some things ta wash up wit in the corner. Courtesy o' the master."

After that pronouncement, the two men scurried back up the staircase.

"How long must we stay here?" Phillip called after them.

"Until the master arrives," came Beefy's unsatisfying reply.

"Who's the mast—?" Phillip attempted just before the cellar door slammed shut, darkening the room further.

The unmistakable sound of a key being turned in a lock followed.

Phillip stood there and blinked at Sophie. He was still tied at the wrists and ankles while Sophie was only tied at the ankles. She immediately lowered herself to sit on the dirt floor and began tearing at her ankle ropes. It took her a few minutes to free one foot, and she kicked the rope away from the other. Without saying a word, she jumped up and ran toward the stairs, grabbed the lantern, and began searching the room.

"What are you looking for?" Phillip asked, staring at her calmly.

"A knife, or something to cut your ties," she replied, without slowing down or stopping her search.

"There should be a knife hanging on the wall near that barrel, over by the flour sacks," he said, nodding toward the space.

She stopped immediately and frowned, turning slowly to look at him. "How do you know?"

"I know because when I was a child, I used to play here daily. We're in the cellar at Graystone Manor, the Harlowe ancestral estate."

CHAPTER TWENTY-ONE

Sophie stood close to Phillip while she cut off his wrist ties. Even though they'd just spent the night rolling around in a questionably clean coach, he still smelled good. And how the man managed to look barely mussed after being kidnapped at knifepoint she would *never* know, but he had accomplished both. The slight stubble that had grown on his face only served to make him look a bit roguish and dangerously handsome. Good heavens. How could she be thinking such thoughts when they were clearly in danger? She needed to focus.

"If this is Graystone Manor," she breathed, trying to reconcile that fact with their abduction, "then..."

"Hugh is almost certainly a part of this," Phillip finished for her. "And there's no doubt as to our location. I knew the moment we entered the house. I'd recognize that specific mixture of the housekeeper's rosemary and mint cleaning oil anywhere. It's Mrs. Jarvis's special concoction."

Sophie nodded. It wasn't particularly surprising that Hugh was part of whatever was going on, but who was he working with? Who was the man she'd heard in the salon with Valentina? Not that it mattered at the moment. The only thing that mattered now was finding a way out of here. The cellar wasn't as close as a carriage, but the ceiling was low and the space made her uneasy. Not to mention, even if men from the Home Office had followed them, there was no guarantee they'd be saved.

As soon as Phillip's wrists were free, Sophie left him to remove his own ankle ropes while she continued to search the room.

"What are you looking for now?" Phillip called after her.

"Another way out," she replied without pausing her search.

"I'm afraid the door we came in is the only way out, and it's quite sturdy when locked, believe me. Malcolm locked me in on enough occasions for me to become an expert on the subject."

Sophie came back to stand in the center of the room near Phillip, still holding the lantern. She expelled a deep breath. "Damn it."

Phillip's brows shot up. "Cursing, my lady? Is the situation so dire?"

She turned to him, an incredulous look on her face. "Isn't it? We need to find a way out of here. Let's get started."

"There's no use," Phillip replied, turning slowly in a circle. "This room has thick stone walls and no windows. The door is solid wood, and the lock is huge, from what I recall."

Sophie nearly stamped her foot. "Fine. What do you suggest, then?"

Phillip shrugged. "I suggest we stay here until 'master' arrives."

"But we already deduced that Master is clearly Hugh," she said, exasperated. "Who else would bring us to Graystone Manor?"

Phillip shrugged. "I'm certain Hugh's a part of it and

whatever is meant to happen here is supposed to result in my death."

Sophie eyed him warily. "You seem far too cheerful to have just said that." She shook her head, her brow furrowed. "If you think they're going to kill you, why won't you help me find a way out?"

Phillip shrugged again. "Because I want to know who else is a part of this. I want to know who you heard speaking to your stepmother."

"Well, then, we disagree, because I'd rather not remain here and find out, and I think you're mad for wanting to stay."

Phillip grinned at her. "I want to know who killed my brother, and I have a feeling if I remain here long enough, I will find out."

Sophie blew air into her cheeks before slowing releasing it. The man had obviously gone mad. Perhaps the blow to his head had been worse than she'd thought. "That's your plan? Stay and be murdered?"

"I never said I intended to allow them to murder me," he replied with a chuckle.

"Fine. You sit around and wait for them to decide your fate. I'm going to try to get that door open." She hoisted the lantern into the air and determinedly climbed up the stairs.

NEARLY AN HOUR LATER, Sophie had given up her attempt to open the blasted door. It was made of rock as far as she was concerned. She tried everything she could think of, including slamming her body against it, kicking it, and cursing it. Nothing seemed to make it budge, and she'd only managed to rip a hole in her rumpled skirts.

She had made enough of a racket that the smaller of the

two men who'd abducted them came back. She convinced him to take her to use the convenience. But afterward, he escorted her right back to the cellar door and ushered her inside.

Disheartened, she trudged back down the stairs to see Phillip sitting on the only piece of furniture available, a small cot near the wall of wine. He was using a rock to sharpen the knife they'd used to remove his ties. God-knew-where he'd found a rock. Sophie made her way to the middle of the dusty room, where she sat next to Phillip. The moment her bottom touched the mattress, an overwhelming feeling of tiredness came over her and she let out a long, loud sigh. Phillip set the knife and rock on the ground and put an arm around her, pulling her softly to cradle her against his side. She tipped toward him. Reveling in the feel of his muscular arms around her, a sense of safety enveloped her. She closed her eyes and drifted off to sleep in the embrace of the only man she'd ever loved.

SOPHIE SLOWLY LIFTED herself from the cot and stretched. Good heavens. She'd fallen asleep. The thin lumpy bed was hardly the sort of accommodation she was used to, and after the uncomfortable coach ride and the distress she was under, it surprised her she'd been able to sleep at all. But she couldn't deny that she felt rested. How long had she been asleep? The darkness in the room gave no hint as to the time. It could be afternoon. It could be evening.

Blinking, she glanced around the large space. The lantern was still burning by the bedside, casting a dull glow across the room. Where was Phillip? She frowned. He was nowhere to be seen and the knife and rock appeared to be gone, too. Fear spiked through her middle. Had they come to get him while she'd been sleeping? Had Phillip already met with harm? Had Hugh killed him like he had Malcolm? Another horrible thought followed quickly on the heels of the first. She might well be in danger herself. If they did intend to kill Phillip, or already had, she would be a witness. She'd merely been at the wrong place at the wrong time and been abducted with Phillip accidentally. Hadn't she? What could Hugh possibly want with her?

A man's voice drifted through the floorboards from above. She froze and held her breath, listening intently to hear his words.

"You are an imbecile. I should have managed all of this myself."

Sophie gasped and quickly clasped her hand over her mouth to muffle the sound. She recognized that voice. It was the same one that had been speaking to Valentina in Papa's salon. Sophie still didn't know who it belonged to, however. Was it Lord Vining? Perhaps. She still couldn't be certain.

"How was I to know they would take Sophia too?" came Hugh's wheedling voice. *That* voice she would know anywhere.

"You should have made it clear!" came the first man's voice.

Just then, Phillip emerged from the darkness at the back of the room. Sophie's eyes flew wide. She hadn't seen him before. He had been hidden in the shadows. Sleeping too, perhaps? He opened his mouth as if he was about to speak, but she held up a finger in front of her mouth to indicate silence. Then she pointed to the ceiling.

Phillip strode forward quickly and they both stood together, listening.

"I told them to take Phillip," Hugh's voice continued, still petulant. "I never mentioned Sophia. How was I to know she'd be there?"

Phillip arched a brow. The look on his face indicated that he, too, recognized his cousin's annoying tone.

"You knew she'd be there because I *told you* she would," came the other man's voice. "You read the note Roberts showed us. She asked him to meet her in the park."

Sophie gasped again before quickly whispering to Phillip, "Roberts is Valentina's awful butler." Sophie narrowed her eyes. If she lived through this, she would find a way to kick that hideous man out on his arse for his betrayal.

"What's done is done," Hugh replied. "The question is, what are we going to do now?"

"We don't have any choice, you fool," came the first voice. "We must kill them both."

CHAPTER TWENTY-TWO

P hillip expelled his breath. Hugh was upstairs, but *who* was he talking to? Phillip couldn't place the second man's voice. It sounded vaguely familiar to him, too. Could it be the unknown man Sophie had heard her stepmother speaking to? Was it Lord Vining? He'd only spoken to Vining for a few minutes at the Cranberrys' ball. And his voice had sounded anxious and weak, nothing like this voice.

Damn it all to hell. The look of stark terror on Sophie's face when the voice had uttered the word 'kill' a few moments ago had made Phillip doubt the logic of his plan. He hated to see her so frightened. Perhaps he should have taken Sophie to safety first. But then their captors might discover her gone and think she'd run away to get help.

Meanwhile, Sophie had gone pale and sank to the cot. She sat staring at the wall as if in a trance. "Did you hear that?" she breathed, gesturing upstairs with one hand.

Phillip nodded. "The first voice is Hugh's. Whose is the other?"

She startled out of her trance and shook herself. Frustration quickly replacing the fear on her face. "I don't know. I still can't place it."

Phillip lowered himself to the cot to sit next to her. He squeezed her hand. "I can't quite place that voice either. Though I'm certain I've heard it before."

Hugh's wheedling tone sounded through the floorboards again. "Do you plan to go down there and shoot them both right now?" This time, there was obvious fright in his voice.

Sophie sprang up as if to run or hide. Phillip's hand grabbed her arm to still her. "Wait," he whispered.

She uneasily lowered herself back to the cot to listen to the rest of the men's conversation.

"No," came the first man's reply. "We can't go off half-cocked. We must make a plan. This has become far too complicated. I've already sent a note. The Jackal will arrive in the morning. Tomorrow will be soon enough."

"Tomorrow," Sophie breathed after the two men had walked off, their footsteps echoing on the floorboards above. "They're going to kill us tomorrow."

"I won't allow anything to happen to you," Phillip promised, squeezing her hand. He looked her deep in the eyes, wanting her to believe she could trust him to keep her safe. "I give you my word."

Sophie nodded. "I hate being confined to this cellar."

Phillip met her gaze, his countenance solemn. "I'm sorry, Sophie. Close your eyes. Pretend you're anywhere else but here."

She managed a smile for him and promptly did. "Very well. I'm in a rowboat in the middle of a pretty lake. Now, what are we going to do?"

Phillip stood and paced away from her. "That second voice, was it the same one you heard talking to your stepmother?"

She nodded vigorously, her eyes still closed. "Yes, I'm certain of it."

Phillip planted his fists on his hips. "I suspected as much. You need to tell me everything you know about Hugh and his friends in London."

"Very well," Sophie replied, taking a deep breath, "but I can tell you right now, I've never heard of anyone called The Jackal."

CHAPTER TWENTY-THREE

Earlier that afternoon, while Sophie was sleeping, Phillip had moved the flour sacks in front of the hidden door in the shadowed part of the cellar and climbed up the small staircase that had been his favorite place to hide as a child. The space seemed tiny now. He'd barely squeezed through it. It had taken all his resolve to breathe—*Three. Two. One.*—as he'd climbed through the close passageway.

Once at the top, he'd pushed up the trapdoor set into the floorboards in one of the empty storage rooms in the kitchen and made his way stealthily through the servants' hall until he'd come to Mrs. Jarvis's office. The imposing lady had a desk inside, from which she ruled the house alongside the butler.

Phillip had stolen into the room and put his finger to his lips to keep Mrs. Jarvis silent. He let his gaze rove over his old friend. The housekeeper had more gray hair than he remembered and perhaps a few more lines near her mouth. Her familiar dark eyes had filled with tears the moment she'd looked up and seen him. "It's true?" she'd whispered. "The rumors are true. Yer alive, and yer back."

Phillip had nodded and come around the desk to envelop the housekeeper in a big hug. The tiny woman smelled just like the same rosemary and mint that pervaded the house. Familiar and wonderful.

"I cannot explain everything now," he'd told her quietly. "But suffice it to say that no one can know I'm here with you. I need you to find the most discreet footman and give him a note." Phillip strode around to the front of her desk, took out a quill and parchment, and leaned over to scribble out some lines before signing it and sealing it with a bit of wax also on the desk. He handed the note to the housekeeper. "This must go directly to London and be placed in the hands of the Marquess of Bellingham immediately. My life depends on it. Do you understand, Mrs. Jarvis?"

The older woman swallowed audibly but nodded. "I do, er...Yer Grace."

A lump formed in Phillip's throat at the mention of his title, and he exchanged an emotion-filled glance with the woman. They were both thinking of Malcolm. He knew it. "Thank you, Mrs. Jarvis."

Mrs. Jarvis gave her head a shake. "Please tell me yer gonna get rid o' that lout who's been making a mockery o' the Harlowe name. He told me the rumors about yer return were untrue. He told me it was an imposter trying ta claim the title."

"Don't worry." Phillip grinned at her. "I intend to rid us *all* of that lout at my first opportunity, Mrs. Jarvis."

"Good," the housekeeper said with a snort, her hands placed firmly on her hips.

"One more question," Phillip replied. "Who is the man here with Hugh? His dinner guest."

The housekeeper shook her head. "Never seen him before

in me life. And that excuse fer a cousin o' yers didn't even have the decency ta introduce him ta me. Been calling him 'me lord' all this time."

Phillip cursed under his breath. "Very well. Thank you, Mrs. Jarvis. Remember, tell *no one* that you've seen me."

"Ye can count on it, Yer Grace," the woman replied with a wink, holding up the note he'd given her. "I'll get this out right quick."

Phillip returned to the small kitchen storage room and climbed through the door in the floorboards, forcing himself to concentrate on his breaths as he traveled back through the tight passageway.

He'd contemplated not going back to the cellar. He didn't have to. He could simply call down for Sophie to join him—he knew she could make it through the tight passage if she had to. She could close her eyes. He would help her. They could go directly to the stables, get a mount, and leave. But whatever was about to unfold in the next day would finally give him the answers he sought regarding Malcolm's death. And if Phillip left too soon, he might never learn the identity of Hugh's cohorts. Phillip refused to let anyone involved in Malcolm's death go free. No. Phillip would stay and play out this little charade. He wasn't afraid of Hugh, and he never would be. Not to mention, he needed to know the identity of the other man upstairs. *And* the mysterious Jackal.

Two hours after Phillip and Sophie had heard the unsettling conversation between Hugh and his guest, Phillip had cobbled together a makeshift dinner for himself and Sophie out of supplies he found in the cellar, including some cheese, cured meat, and bread. He'd even cracked open a bottle of the finest wine, which they drank sitting side-by-side on the cot. Sophie had taken off her cape and draped it over the cot.

At first, they ate in silence, ravenous after realizing they hadn't eaten in nearly an entire day. But after they'd both had their fill and consumed nearly three quarters of the bottle of wine, Sophie took another swig and said, "I've been filled with dread all afternoon. Funny how wine makes it all seem more ridiculous than dangerous."

"I won't let any harm come to you, Sophie. I meant that."

Sophie took yet another drink from the wine bottle. "Oh, yes. Why should I be worried about being harmed? There are only two men upstairs with pistols who plan to murder us in the morning." Irony dripped from her voice.

Phillip took the bottle from her and took a long drink before handing it back to her. He had already decided. If they ran out of time, he would tell her about the passageway. Send her to safety while he met his fate. *Not* that he intended to allow Hugh, of all people, to harm him. But he had to be prepared to keep Sophie safe.

For now, he would settle for distracting her from worrying about their fate. Phillip bumped his knee against hers. "Tell me something."

Sophie blinked. A smile popped to her lips. She took another drink from the bottle. "What do you mean? What do you want to know?"

Phillip pulled the bottle from her fingers and took a swig again. "Tell me everything I missed. The last year of your life."

Sophie swallowed and stared into the darkness on the far side of the room for a few moments. "There's not much to tell, really."

"Come now, that can't be true," Phillip prodded. "You must have done *something* these last months."

Sophie's gaze dropped to the floor. When she looked up again, her eyes were filled with tears.

"Sophie—" he began. *Damn it.* He hadn't meant to make her sad. He'd merely wanted to change the subject.

She shook her head. "You told me once that you were broken," she began softly.

Phillip nodded solemnly, setting the wine bottle on the floor between their feet. He pulled his handkerchief from his pocket and handed it to her.

"Well, I was broken too," Sophie breathed, accepting the handkerchief. "You've no idea what it was like for me the day I heard you were dead. I died that day, too." Her voice faltered. "I died inside."

A lump lodged itself in Phillip's throat as he reached out to stroke her hair. "Sophie, I…"

She bit her trembling lip, a faraway look in her eyes. "My body may still have been walking around, my heart may still have been pumping blood. But I was gone."

"I'm sorry," he breathed. "So damn sorry." His hand moved down to stroke her back.

Sophie took another shaky breath. "Those first weeks, months after I believed you had died, Phillip, they were a blur. I felt completely empty inside. I didn't go out, didn't talk, couldn't eat. I gave up hope for a happy life."

Phillip forced himself to swallow the lump in his throat. "You've always been so positive, Sophie. I can't imagine *you* giving up hope."

The ghost of a smile passed over her lips. She met his gaze. "Did I ever tell you why I was always so positive?"

He shook his head. "I only know that the moment I met you, I felt as if the sun was shining on me."

Another hint of a smile graced her lips before she lifted the wine bottle and took a sip. "You know my mama died when I was a girl."

Phillip nodded.

"She'd been sick for months," Sophie continued. "When it was time, I went to her bedside to say goodbye. I was sobbing. I told her I wanted to go with her. I told her I didn't want to be here without her." Tears slipped down Sophie's face. She dabbed at them with the handkerchief.

Phillip's eyes misted. He swallowed again.

"You know what Mama replied?" Sophie asked him, her voice a mere whisper.

"No," he managed past his clogged throat.

"She told me that everyone has two choices in their life every single day, no matter what happens to them." She took a deep breath. "The first choice is to be sad, to complain, to wonder why anything bad happens." Another breath. "The second is to be happy, to see the good in everyone and everything, to decide that whatever comes, life is worth living."

Phillip swallowed and nodded again.

Sophie swiped at the tears on her cheeks with the handkerchief. "Mama told me to make certain I didn't become a sad, complaining person. She told me to ensure I woke up every morning and *chose* to be happy, because the things that come will come either way and it's up to me to either embrace them with hope or curse them with hopelessness."

"You chose hope," Phillip murmured.

Sophie nodded and set the bottle back on the ground. "I chose it every day. Even when I didn't get my way, or skinned my knee, or felt as if I was all alone. Even when Papa married Valentina and she was hideous to me. I chose to be happy because that's what Mama wanted for me."

Phillip reached down and squeezed her hand. His heart was in a vise. It hurt so much to hear these words, but he had no doubt it had hurt her much more to live through it.

Her brown eyes remained shiny with tears. "But Phillip, for months after I thought you were dead, I didn't choose to

147

be happy." She shook her head. "There was no choice left for me. I couldn't even remember what happy felt like."

Expelling his pent-up breath, Phillip pulled her into his arms and hugged her fiercely, whispering in her ear, "Oh, Sophie, I'm sorry. I'm sorry I did that to you. I'm sorry I made you experience that grief once again. As long as I live, I'll never forgive myself."

When they pulled apart, Sophie continued, closing her eyes as if struggling with the memories. "I want you to know...by the time Valentina announced my engagement to Hugh, I didn't care if I ever married, let alone to who. It was all just a blur. I only wanted her to stop pestering me to become betrothed."

Sophie straightened her shoulders and lifted her chin. "Everything after you was just fog, Phillip. It was all nothingness." She turned her head slightly to meet his gaze, her eyes slightly red from crying.

Phillip leaned forward and pressed his forehead to hers. "I know there's nothing I can ever do to make it up to you, but—"

His words were silenced as Sophie tilted her chin forward and pressed her lips against his. The moment she did, Phillip tugged her into his arms and slanted his mouth across hers. She tasted like wine. She felt like heaven in his arms. He'd missed her so much. He'd loved her for years. And he was beyond sorry for the pain he'd caused her.

"Sophie," he whispered, pulling his mouth from hers and kissing her temple, her cheek, her jaw. "Sophie." He breathed in the scent of her hair and wiped his thumbs across her wet cheeks, kissing her again. "Please don't cry. I'll never make you cry again."

In response, Sophie wrapped her arms around his neck and kissed him fiercely.

A few minutes later, he pulled his mouth from hers and

rested his forehead against hers again, his breathing still heavy from their kissing. "Do you still love me, Sophie?"

The hint of a smile lifted her lips, and she dabbed at her nose with the handkerchief. "Of course I do, you idiot."

"I love you, too," he breathed. "I never stopped." He reached up and stroked her cheek with the back of his hand.

She pulled her forehead from his and sat up straight, expelling her breath and folding the handkerchief on her lap. She was no longer crying. "I deserve to know the truth," she said in a strong, clear voice. "What happened in Devon, Phillip? Why do you think you would no longer make a good husband?"

Phillip nodded slowly. It was time. "What I told you was true...partially. I *was* badly injured physically and—" His breath caught in his throat. Now that the moment had come, he couldn't seem to force the words past his lips.

"And what?" She searched his face. "You must tell me, Phillip. What happened to you? What was so bad to make you think you're unworthy of my love?"

Phillip hung his head. Then he took her hand and intertwined his fingers with hers. "My illness...it wasn't just physical." He took a deep breath. "There was something wrong with my *mind* as well." He lifted his head again to see her reaction.

Her brow was furrowed. "Your mind? What do you mean?"

Phillip took another deep breath. His lungs hurt. His heart hurt. This was it. It was time to tell Sophie the entire truth. She was correct. She deserved it. She had always deserved it. "I couldn't speak. I had constant dreams of bloodshed and battlefields. I still have them, Sophie. I can't escape them."

Pain slashed across her features as Sophie lifted a hand

149

and placed it on his cheek. "Oh, Phillip," she breathed. "I'm sorry."

He lifted his gaze toward the ceiling, shaking his head. "I couldn't return to Society that way, and I wasn't certain I would ever recover. I stayed away. I let everyone think I was dead."

More pain flashed across Sophie's pretty face. "That's what you didn't want to tell me?"

He nodded. "I was afraid you'd think I'd gone mad. Who would want to marry a man who couldn't speak? I...I was no longer the same man you met three years ago. I never will be. The war...changed me. There's no telling whether it might happen again."

She pulled her hand away from his cheek, wrapped her arms around his neck again, and hugged him tightly. "I still would have wanted to marry you, Phillip. I promise you."

His eyes stung with unshed tears, but he hugged her back, saying, "It isn't normal to be unable to speak. It was...mortifying. If I had been stronger, I—"

Sophie pulled away from him, but grabbed both of his hands and squeezed them. She looked him straight in the eye. "Phillip, you saw the worst things imaginable. You nearly *died*. You're not mad...you're human. You simply needed time. You still need time."

More tears pricked the back of Phillip's eyes. Pain and regret slashed through his chest. He should have known that Sophie, his darling Sophie, would accept whatever shortcomings he had. She had never let him down before. Which made it even worse that he'd ever doubted her. "I'll never be able to forgive myself," he breathed. "For so many things..."

She searched his face. "What? What other things?"

He took another deep breath. His next words would be the most difficult he'd ever spoken in his life. He had never said them aloud before. Not to Clayton, not to Bell, not even to Thea. Phillip hung his head and clenched his jaw. His voice was raw. "If I'd had the strength to face what had happened to me...if I hadn't broken...Malcolm would still be alive."

"What?" Sophie continued to search his face, confusion written all over her features. "What do you mean, Phillip? You cannot possibly truly believe that."

Phillip took another painful breath. He swallowed hard. "Hugh obviously killed Malcolm to gain the title because he believed I was already dead. And I let him believe it by being too weak to come forward."

"What? No!" Sophie replied, shaking her head so vehemently her curls bounced. Horror and denial were combined on her face. She squeezed both of his hands again. "Phillip, you *cannot* blame yourself. You had every right to take the time to heal the way you needed to from the atrocities you experienced. You're not responsible for the actions of another. How could you ever think that?"

Phillip closed his eyes and clasped Sophie's hands with his more tightly. An unfamiliar feeling of relief swept through him. What Sophie said made sense. For the first time in what felt like forever, he felt a modicum of peace. He'd never considered it that way before. He'd been far too preoccupied with his guilt. "Thank you, Sophie. I think I've needed to hear that for quite a long time." He tugged her into another hug and whispered into her ear, "Thank you for helping me to see the world differently. You've always been good at that."

"You're welcome." They kissed once more before Sophie pulled away and asked, "Now. Do you think Lord Vining will be the Jackal?"

"Are you trying to distract me, Miss?" he asked with a laugh.

"Yes," she replied, smiling.

"I don't know if Vining is the Jackal or the man upstairs." Phillip rubbed his jaw. "I suppose we'll find out in the morning."

"Speaking of the morning," Sophie continued, "you seem awfully certain and calm for someone who is about to be killed."

A half-grin, half-guilty look stretched across Phillip's face. "There's something I haven't told you yet."

Sophie arched a brow. "What's that?"

"I know a secret way out of this cellar."

CHAPTER TWENTY-FOUR

Sophie jumped up, nearly stumbling off the cot. "You know a way to get out of here?" she nearly shouted. "Why didn't you tell me?"

Phillip winced and bit his lip. "Two reasons. First, the way out is a *very* tight space."

He watched as Sophie frowned at that news.

"And second," he continued, "I wanted to be certain that I could still make it through, that it hadn't been sealed, before I lifted your hopes."

"Well?" she asked. "Did you check it? Is it still open?"

"Yes," Phillip replied with a solid nod. "And I always intended to tell you. Especially if things go wrong."

"Well, we won't have to worry about that anymore, will we?" Sophie jumped up. "Let's go. I'll do what I must to get through the small space." She turned in a circle, clearly eager to locate the door and escape. "Where is it?"

"We can't leave yet," Phillip said simply.

Sophie whirled to face him. "What? Why? Didn't you hear them, Phillip? They are going to *kill* us."

"They *want* to kill us," Phillip replied. "That's very different from actually accomplishing it."

Sophie crossed her arms over her chest and gave him a stern stare. "I don't understand. Why would we possibly stay?"

Phillip stood. "Because I'm tired of playing games with Hugh. I vowed when I came back to town, I'd be strong enough to fight for Malcolm's memory and I am. I'm not about to go running off to hide now. I want to know once and for all what happened to my brother, and I want to know the identities of everyone who was involved."

Sophie expelled her breath and walked back over to where Phillip stood. She placed a hand on his shoulder. "I can understand that, but can't we go fetch the constable first? He can arrest Hugh and whoever is helping him and question them."

Phillip cracked a grin. "I have someone even better than the constable already on the way. While you were sleeping, I went upstairs and sent word to Bell. He should be here before dawn breaks."

Sophie eyed him warily. "I thought you said the Home Office followed us here. If they were going to rescue us, I'd have thought they'd done so by now."

Phillip winced and rubbed the back of his neck. "There's something else I never told you."

She put her fists on her hips and glared at him. "What?"

"I slipped away from the men from the Home Office who were following me the night I met you in the park. They were never coming. Until now, that is. I'm sorry. I didn't want you to be frightened."

Sophie closed her eyes and leaned her head back. "I'm relieved to hear that they're coming now, but are you certain staying here is the best way to handle it? They have at least one pistol, Phillip."

"Bell will bring more pistols. I have a knife, and we have a way out if we need to use it. But if you want to go, Sophie, I'll help you through. I don't want to put you in danger."

Sophie contemplated the matter for a moment, tapping her finger against her chin. "No. We either stay together or leave together. I won't leave you, Phillip. Besides, if they come to check on us and I'm gone, they'll know we have a way out."

"Trust me. This will all be over soon enough." Phillip sauntered over to the wall of wine bottles and picked another Madeira. "The only thing left to do is to drink a bit more and see if we can't recall whose voice that is."

Sophie shook her head. "You really *aren't* worried about this, are you?"

"I've taken precautions," Phillip replied, pulling the cork from the bottle he'd chosen. "You must believe me when I say I will let nothing happen to you. Or to my mother's only remaining son. She would never forgive me."

Sophie took a seat on the cot once again. "Very well." She held out her hand. "Then pass the wine."

He made his way to the cot and handed her the bottle before taking a seat next to her again. Sophie took a long swig, then smiled at him. "I know you're confident about our being safe down here, but there *is* a possibility something might go wrong and we *may* end up dead."

"No." Phillip firmly shook his head.

"A slight possibility, you must admit," she prodded.

"No." Phillip continued shaking.

"Agree with me, you infuriating man. I'm trying to make a point."

"Fine. A very tiny, minute possibility," he allowed, grinning back at her.

She took another swig from the wine bottle. "Then I want you to do something for me tonight."

He eyed her carefully from the sides of his eyes. "What's that?"

She took a deep breath. She'd made her decision, and she was certain of it. She did not know what tomorrow would bring, let alone tonight, but she wanted to do this no matter what. "I don't want to die a virgin."

CHAPTER TWENTY-FIVE

A thousand thoughts raced through Phillip's head at once. What had Sophie just said? Dear God. Precisely what he thought she'd just said. He took a deep, shuddering breath. "Sophie, we can't—"

Sophie leaned forward and put her free arm around his neck. "Please, Phillip. We don't know what will happen in the morning."

Facing her, he squeezed her sides while he searched her beautiful face. "That's not a good enough rationale for me to..." He needed to be the one who displayed reason here, didn't he? He needed to be the one who realized why this was a ludicrous idea. Hadn't he just finished telling her they'd be safe? Her logic wasn't sound. She'd regret this tomorrow.

Sophie pushed herself away from his chest, eyeing him carefully, her features filled with apprehension. "Please don't tell me you don't want me. Tell me anything but that."

"Of course I want you. I've always wanted you." He scrubbed a hand through his hair. Damn it all to hell. Were they actually having this conversation? Was this truly happening? His most cherished dream through all the long months on battlefields and the torturous months recovering had been taking Sophie to his bed, making her his. How could she ever possibly think he didn't want her?

A triumphant smile spread across Sophie's face, and she took another drink from the bottle. "And I've always wanted you, too. Don't you see? It's the perfect time."

"Sophie, I wish—"

"I wish too. Why are we still wishing when we're here now?"

Phillip continued to shake his head. "But I still can't promise you—"

She put a finger to his lips to silence him. "I'm not asking for promises. I'm only asking for a night."

Phillip's mind raced. How could he make her see reason? She was entrusted to his care. She was frightened, and she was vulnerable. He was not about to take advantage of her. No matter how much he truly wanted her. "No. No. No," he said. "And that's an end to it."

PHILLIP WOKE in the middle of the night to Sophie's soft, warm body pressed against him. After calling him a scoundrel for refusing to make love to her, she'd insisted they sleep next to each other on the small cot. It was the only place to sleep; she reasoned. He hadn't been able to think of an excuse to refuse her, knowing he might never have the opportunity to spend a night by her side again.

She'd removed her gown and stays and was wearing only her shift. They'd used her cape as their only blanket. Her backside was pressed close to his groin and was rubbing against him in a way that made him ache. He moved away from her when she flipped over in her sleep and flung an arm across his shoulder. She let out a breathy moan that instantly made him rock-hard.

He swallowed. She snuggled closer, her full breasts pressing tightly against his chest. Her hand traveled down his side to rest on his hip.

Wait a minute. Was she actually sleeping?

"Sophie?" he whispered.

"Mmm hmm," she whispered back.

"What are you doing?"

"Trying to seduce you."

Phillip froze. It felt as if the darkened room was closing in on him. At the same time, it felt as if his greatest dream was coming true. He'd wanted Sophie for so long. Only he'd thought he would make love to her on their wedding night. Now there was little chance of that.

Phillip closed his eyes, and in that moment, he gave up the fight to resist her. There was really no choice to make at all. He'd loved her for so long.

"Are you certain that's what you want?" he breathed against her lips.

"Yes," she whispered back, wrapping both arms around his neck, and pulling herself to splay fully against his body.

Phillip closed his eyes. All they had was tonight. He would make love to her.

WHEN PHILLIP'S hand drifted down her side to the bottom of her shift, Sophie smiled to herself. She had won. They were going to do this. And she wanted it…badly. There were people with pistols upstairs and no surety that they would be saved.

Besides the soul-numbing fear, there was a certain reckless freedom in thinking you might well only have hours left to live. Absolutely nothing mattered...like the consequences of no longer being a virgin. It was silly how highly their Society valued a thing like virginity. What in the world did it matter when one faced death? In the three long years she'd waited for Phillip, Sophie had fantasized about their wedding night over and over. There hadn't been a wedding and there probably never would be, but they could still do this. And she intended to enjoy every moment.

Before they'd retired for the night, she'd enlisted Phillip's help to remove her gown and stays. She'd been quite calculating, really, when it came to convincing him to make love to her. Once they were in bed and pressed against each other, fate was on her side. It had only been a matter of time before Phillip could no longer resist. Sophie had counted on it.

Phillip's warm hand slowly pulled her shift up to her bare hip. He stroked her upper thigh with the backs of his fingers. Then he moved his hand around to her backside and pulled her thigh up over one of his. Sophie gasped. She wanted his hand where she ached. Deep between her legs.

He smoothed his hand down over her knee, then back up to her hip before drifting it inexorably toward the juncture between her legs. He stroked her once, twice, and she cried out, mostly from the delicious friction from his hand. His fingers played with her, rubbed her, moved along her seam before he smoothed one long finger inside of her. Sophie sucked in her breath and clutched his broad shoulders. He moved his finger slowly inside of her. Her breathing quickened.

"Sophie," he whispered against her ear. "How much do you know about this?"

"Ab...absolutely nothing," she gasped as he continued to stroke her.

He nibbled at her ear and then let his tongue delve inside.

She whimpered, her hips undulating against the steady rhythm of his hand.

"You're so hot and wet," he whispered. "That means you're ready for me."

Sophie let her head fall back. "I've been ready for you for three years."

She felt his smile against her cheek. He kissed her ear, her neck, her shoulder, all while still stroking her gently with his finger inside. "What I'm doing...with my finger," he finally managed, "I will do with me."

"You?" she asked somewhat mindlessly, not entirely certain what he was saying.

"Yes," he answered, pulling one of her hands from his shoulder and placing it between his legs so she could feel his erection beneath his breeches.

"Ooh," she said, shuddering. "*You.*"

"Yes." He replied, pulling his finger away from her most intimate spot. "It may be...uncomfortable for you at first."

"How...uncomfortable?" Sophie asked, her hips still moving, wanting his finger back.

"I hope not much," he replied.

"Is it uncomfortable for you, too?" she asked, frowning.

He chuckled and kissed her on the forehead. "No. Unfair, I know."

Sophie frowned. "Does it *remain* uncomfortable?"

"God, I hope not," Phillip replied, chuckling again. "I hope it feels better than when I was touching you just now."

"Better?" Sophie asked, her brows lifting.

Phillip nodded. "Mmm. Hmm."

"Then what are you waiting for?"

Phillip chuckled a third time. "Not a bad point." He rolled off the cot and stood, while Sophie moved to the opposite side of the small bed and lit the lantern. She rolled back to face him again and lifted on her elbow to watch in the soft glow of light while he removed his shirt with both hands behind his head. His chest was magnificent, smooth and muscled, his shoulders wide. She frowned when she saw the scar on one shoulder. That's where the shot had hit him. She didn't have long to contemplate it, however, because he soon unbuttoned his breeches and pulled them off.

She gasped when she saw his member, proud and strong, jutting out from the hair between his legs. It was bigger than she'd imagined. She wanted to touch him.

"Now you," he breathed, reaching down to help her stand.

Phillip pulled her up beside him, and Sophie took a deep, shuddering breath. She reached down and pulled up her shift from her knees, over her hips, torso, and head and tossed it onto the floor near the cot. They stood staring at each other's naked bodies for several moments, neither saying a word.

"You're perfect, Sophie," Phillip finally breathed, reaching out and touching her shoulders, her arms.

"You are too," Sophie replied. She tentatively touched Phillip's broad shoulders. She stopped at the jagged scar on his upper chest. "Does it hurt?" she asked, wincing.

"Not anymore," he replied. His hand had moved to her breasts, and he leaned down and kissed each one before moving his hand down to smooth over her flat abdomen. "You're beautiful. Do you know that?"

She shook her head. "Not as beautiful as you are," she replied, letting her palm skim down his muscled chest in much the same manner.

He moved his hands to her hips and pulled her closer while she let her fingers move around his back to press against his firm buttocks. Then she boldly wrapped the other hand around his cock and squeezed.

Phillip sucked in his breath.

"Do you like that?" she asked, looking up at him, a wicked smile on her lips.

"It's like torture," he breathed, smiling at her. "The best kind of torture."

She moved to squeeze him again, but Phillip scooped her up into his arms and laid her on the cot. Then he lowered himself atop her. He kissed her mouth, long and loving, exploring every inch. She still tasted like wine. His lips moved to her cheek, her ear, and her neck, before his head moved down to take one of her nipples into his mouth.

Sophie cried out and arched her back, calling his name. Her fingers tangled in his hair.

He gently bit her nipple, rolling it around with his tongue and teeth before sucking it, pulling on it, making her gasp. Desire shot through her. The ache between her legs intensified.

He moved his mouth to her other breast and the roughness of the stubble on his face rubbed against her soft skin, driving her mad. He sucked her nipple and tugged it with his teeth, giving it the same attention as the first. She tried to reach for his cock again, but he moved his hips down, out of her reach.

When he moved even lower, skimming his lips along her ribcage and kissing her belly, all the breath left Sophie's body.

"Phillip, I—"

"Let me taste you, Sophie," he breathed, settling himself between her thighs.

A nod and a half-whimper were her only answer.

Phillip took a deep breath. Here was Sophie, the woman he'd loved, the woman he'd dreamed about, splayed in front of him, naked, giving herself to him entirely. It was more than he deserved. He knew it, and he wanted to make it special for her.

He lowered his mouth to her, dipping his tongue into her slick folds, closing his eyes, and reveling in her sweetness. He licked her over and over as her hands grabbed at his hair and soft whimpering noises issued from her throat. There would nothing more memorable than the sound of Sophie taking her pleasure. And he had barely begun.

His tongue rooted out the sweet nub of hidden flesh, the one that would give her maximum pleasure. He licked her, over and over, rubbing her in tight little circles that made her hips writhe and her hands mindlessly smooth over his shoulders.

"Phillip," she breathed. He loved hearing his name on her lips, especially all breathy and heated as her gratification escalated. "Phillip," she moaned as he licked her again and again, vowing not to stop until he made her come apart.

He brushed his rough tongue against her until her hips lifted from the cot and her knees clamped against his head. Her breaths came in pants, hitching little whimpers that made his cock even harder. And when she finally cried out, little shudders racked her gorgeous body as her hips fell back to the cot and her chest heaved with satisfaction.

After her trembling subsided, Phillip moved back up her body to kiss her lips. She was still breathing heavily and stared up at him in amazement. "What was that?" she asked, eyes wide.

"That was what it feels like when lovemaking is done properly," he said with no small amount of pride.

She stared at him with wide eyes, as if he'd just unlocked the secret of the universe. "You've known about this? Three years ago, even?"

He bit his lip and nodded. "Afraid so."

She playfully slapped at his shoulder. "Phillip, you beast. We should have done this back then!"

Phillip laughed before leaning down and kissing her on the tip of the nose. "I'm afraid your father might have called me out."

"Who cares? We could have been married. We could have —" She broke off, looking sheepish. "There's more, isn't there?"

He nodded.

She dipped her chin to her chest. "For you?"

He nodded again.

This time, before he had a chance to move his hips away, her hand shot down between his legs and wrapped fiercely around his cock. She stroked him once, twice.

He groaned.

"Is this right?" she asked tentatively, still stroking him in an unmerciful pattern that made Phillip's hips pump against her fist.

"Oh, yes," he breathed, bracing himself on his elbows on either side of her head. "Stroke me."

Sophie did as she was told. She drew her hand along his length, reveling in the smooth, hot feel of him. The best part was Phillip's reaction. She watched the emotions play across his handsome face. The more she stroked him, the harder, the faster, the more his breathing skipped and the more sweat beaded on his brow. The more his jaw clenched, the more air he sucked through his gritted teeth. Power and lust combined to flow through her veins as she watched him thrust against her touch, his eyes tightly closed.

"If I keep doing this," she finally whispered. "Will you feel how I felt?"

Phillip couldn't form a word. He could only give her a jerky nod.

"Well, I—"

Her thought was interrupted as Phillip's hand covered hers, forcibly removing it from him. He pinned her hands over her head with his while his breathing settled back to rights.

"Why did you stop me?" she asked, mock-frowning up at him.

"Because, I—" He still needed a moment.

She waited patiently.

"It's not quite the same for a man," he finally managed. "If I feel how you felt, I'll spend my seed and—"

"And?" she prompted, eyeing him carefully.

"And I want to do that inside of you," he answered, nuzzling her neck.

Sophie's mouth formed a wide O before a big smile replaced it.

"That's how children are made," he whispered.

"Oh, yes, of course," she replied, feeling like a ninny for not having realized it before. Mama had died before Sophie had been of an age to discuss such things, and she'd never been able to ask Valentina for the information. Papa, of course, had never offered.

"We're not trying to make a baby, of course," Phillip continued. "But... But I want to feel you, Sophie. I want to be inside of you." He let go of her hands.

"I want that too," she breathed, wrapping her arms tightly around his neck.

Phillip kissed her again, before lowering himself over her and nudging her legs apart with his knee.

She closed her eyes tight, bracing herself for the uncomfortable part. But when Phillip slid inside of her, there was only heat and warmth and fullness and... He began to move, and she forgot her own name.

"Sophie," he whispered into her ear, reminding her. "Are you all right?"

"Yes," she promptly replied, her nails raking lightly across his bare back.

"Wrap your legs around me."

Sophie didn't hesitate. She clapped her legs around his

lower back as he rocked back and forth inside of her, dragging out and sliding back in again and again. It wasn't until he moved one of his hands down to rub her in that same spot where he'd licked her earlier that she realized she was going to feel that way all over again. The rocking of his hips, him rubbing against that spot, his finger nudging her in little circles as he moved in and out of her... It all combined to drive her wild. She clutched at his shoulders, whimpering slightly, feeling as if she was on the precipice of a mountaintop getting higher and higher, closer and closer to...

She let out a keening cry as ripples of pleasure spread through her entire body. Phillip stroked into her a few more times before he, too, shuddered and groaned and called her name into her ear as his entire world shattered into a thousand pieces of pleasure.

He lay atop her, slick and sated, breathing heavily for several moments before pulling out and using his strength to roll over, taking her with him. He cradled her against his chest, stroking her dark hair.

"That was..." she began, but soon realized she could not find the words.

"Yes, it was," he agreed with a smile, still stroking her hair.

They laid there for several minutes, both reveling in their pleasure, before Phillip rolled out from under Sophie, stood, and made his way to the makeshift washstand in the corner. The few items Hugh had seen fit to provide them consisted of a pitcher of water, a bowl, and two cloths. Phillip moistened one of the cloths and brought it back to Sophie, cleaning her between her legs. She took it from him and finished, standing up and pulling her shift back over her head when she was done. Phillip pulled on his breeches but left off his shirt. They laid back down together, and Sophie cuddled against his chest.

"I will never regret that," Sophie said.

"I won't, either," Phillip agreed, kissing the top of her head. "Not as long as I live."

The last thought Sophie had before falling into a blissful, sated slumber was that if she was going to die tomorrow, at least she would have this memory to take to her grave.

CHAPTER TWENTY-SIX

The clanging of the key in the lock above them startled Phillip from his sleep. He quickly woke Sophie while pulling on his shirt. The lantern was still burning. They couldn't have been asleep for longer than a few hours. What were their captors doing coming down in the middle of the night?

To be safe, Sophie had already dressed before she'd fallen asleep, so they were both soon up and standing in front of the cot. They watched the staircase with pounding hearts. Phillip glanced over at Sophie to give her a reassuring nod. The look she gave him made his heart wrench. She was clearly terrified.

"Don't worry," he breathed, giving her cold, shaking hand a comforting squeeze.

"I'm far past worry," she replied, staring up at the top of the staircase as if a monster were about to enter the cellar.

The door swung open, and several pairs of feet began to descend the staircase. When a lantern came into view, icy dread shimmied down Phillip's spine. The first man down the stairs was none other than *Bell*...and his wrists were shackled. Bell gave Phillip an apologetic look, just before Hugh and...*Lord Hillsdale* pushed him the rest of the way down the stairs and into the room.

"Good evening, Your Grace," Hugh sneered. "I thought you'd like to see your visitor." Hugh was holding a pistol and poked it at Bell's back as he said the words.

"Hillsdale," Phillip breathed, unable to tear his gaze from the nobleman. "It was *you*." If Hillsdale was here, then Vining had to be the man they called the Jackal. He had obviously been playing the part of a foolish, sweaty, incompetent when they'd first met, but Vining was clearly the mastermind these two had been waiting for.

Phillip narrowed his eyes at Hillsdale. There was no doubt. Hillsdale had been quite an actor, too. His voice was different. Strident and stentorian. Not at all the same nasally, obsequious drone Phillip remembered from the Cranberrys' ball. Not a wonder neither he nor Sophie hadn't been able to place it.

Bell cleared his throat. "I suppose this answers the question of why you never contacted Phillip to come to Whitehall and work out the issue with the title," the marquess said to Hillsdale with a wide grin on his face.

"And I just remembered whose voice I heard in my stepmother's salon," Sophie whispered from beside Phillip, an apologetic look on her face.

Phillip gave her an ironic smile, and she shrugged.

"Lord Bellingham here has been kind enough to grace us with his presence," Hillsdale said, ignoring their jibes. He, too, carried a pistol. "And he was also kind enough to provide us with shackles. We didn't have any of those until he arrived."

"My pleasure," Bell said, bowing.

"Shut up!" Hugh demanded, frowning fiercely at Bell.

Bell frowned back.

"You might also be interested to hear that we know all about your secret passage out of this cellar," Hillsdale continued, directing his remarks to Phillip.

Sophie gasped.

Phillip kept his face completely blank, but his stomach sank. They had Bell, and if they knew about the passageway from the cellar, it stood to reason the trapdoor was locked or being watched. The situation was becoming more dire by the moment.

Hillsdale's grin turned positively evil. "Our man, Bonham —you remember him from your journey here, no doubt— found the footman you sent to deliver the note to Bellingham. We let him continue, of course. We thought Lord Bellingham might want to join this little party, and the footman wouldn't breathe a word as long as we promised not to harm the housemaid he's been shagging. Imagine our surprise when we found Lord Bellingham here, already hiding in the woods near the house."

Phillip narrowed his eyes on Hillsdale as several thoughts raced through his head. So Bell had already figured out where they were. Bonham was probably the man he'd called Beefy. Had they done anything to Mrs. Jarvis, or had they only intercepted the footman?

"Go on," Bell taunted. "If you're going to shoot us, get it over with."

"Lord Bellingham, please," Sophie cried, fear sounding in her voice.

Phillip narrowed his eyes. He knew Bell well enough to know that he'd said those words for a reason. Bell must believe Hillsdale and Hugh weren't in a hurry to kill the three of them. Why?

"Not so fast," Hugh said. "The Jackal is on the way."

"Shut up, you fool," Hillsdale snapped at Hugh. "Not another word."

"The Jackal," Bell repeated with a snort. "Who, pray tell, is that? What sort of ass calls himself 'the Jackal'? Honestly."

Ignoring Bell, Hillsdale turned back toward Phillip. "We'll be back...in the morning. In the meantime, we've already locked the door to the passage and if you try anything foolish, your friend here will end up dead. We're taking Lord Bellingham with us so you don't get clever together and try to plan an escape."

Phillip cursed under his breath and watched impotently as the three went back up the way they came.

The door had barely shut and locked behind them when Sophie turned to Phillip, her eyes wide with fear. "If they have Lord Bellingham and know about the passage..."

"Then we're in real trouble," Phillip breathed.

CHAPTER TWENTY-SEVEN

A sharp rap on the ceiling above him startled Phillip from a light sleep. Apparently, he'd nodded off sometime after Hillsdale and Hugh had taken Bell back upstairs. Phillip shot up off the cot and glanced around. He ran a hand through his hair and rubbed his eyes. How long had he been asleep? There was no telling, but it was morning. The light coming from under the door at the top of the stairs told him so. He lit the lantern and set it near the staircase.

He glanced back over at the cot. Sophie was sleeping. He didn't want to wake her. Why ruin her slumber just to be confronted with the stark reality that they were still prisoners in a cellar, and no one was coming to help them?

He turned in a circle. He needed to make a plan. All he had to defend them with was one small knife. Hugh and Hillsdale both had pistols. But Phillip would have to make do. He would just—

Wait. He stopped. His arms falling to his sides. Last night, before Hugh and Hillsdale had come down, and again, just now, had been the first time since the battle that he'd slept without nightmares and waking in a cold sweat. He turned to stare at Sophie in awe. A smile covered his face. She truly brought light with her wherever she went. She shined it into the deepest, darkest place. Making love to her had been the best experience of his life, and if anything happened to her today—after he'd refused to escape when they'd had the chance—he would never forgive himself.

Phillip's revery was short-lived as voices and footsteps sounded from above. He held his breath to listen.

"You are a complete numbskull," came a shrill woman's voice.

Phillip cocked his head to the side. Who was *that*? There was no help for it. He gently woke Sophie. Sophie rubbed her eyes and sat up, groggily listening after Phillip silently pointed up, then cupped his ear.

"If you won't get on with it, I will," the woman said next. "Give me the pistol. I'll put a shot in Grayson's skull and one in Bellingham's to match."

"Is that your stepmother?" Phillip asked Sophie in a whisper.

"Yes," Sophie said, nodding, her eyes wide. She was already standing. "Wait. You don't think… *Valentina* is the Jackal?"

"Appears so," Phillip replied, blowing air into his cheeks.

Sophie shuddered. "I always knew Valentina disliked me, but I never thought she'd agree to my *murder*."

Phillip stepped over to Sophie and made fast work of the buttons. "I'm not certain she realizes you're here."

Sophie looked up at him, her brow knitted. "What?"

"I'm not sure they told her." Phillip reached down under the cot and grabbed his knife.

"But why—?"

Sophie cut her remark short when Phillip put a finger to his lips. The lock was being opened. He turned quickly to

Sophie and whispered, "Hide. Hide in the shadows behind me. Against the back wall." He gestured to the far end of the room. "Don't come out. No matter what happens, Sophie. Promise me."

Sophie nodded. She hurried into the shadows just as the door to the cellar opened and the glow of another lantern filtered down the staircase. Sunlight streamed in too. Phillip tucked the knife into the top of his breeches. Then he took a deep breath. One way or other, this would be over soon.

Footsteps clomped down the stairs one after another until Hugh, Hillsdale, and a beautiful woman—whom Phillip could only assume was Sophie's stepmother—stood in front of him.

Hugh was busily looking around the room, obviously searching for Sophie. "Where's—?"

A sharp elbow to the gut from Hillsdale silenced the younger man. That was interesting. Apparently, Hillsdale didn't want Valentina to know Sophie was here. But that was probably a good sign. Perhaps it meant they didn't intend to kill her. Phillip could almost breathe a sigh of relief. But nothing would be certain until this ended.

"I don't believe we've had the pleasure," Phillip quickly said, bowing to Valentina to keep Hugh from saying more.

Valentina arched a black brow and stared at him, cocking her head to one side. "So, *you're* the one who's caused so much trouble. The missing duke."

"One and the same," Phillip replied. "And *you* are?"

Valentina lifted her hand that had been hidden in her purple skirts to reveal a pistol, which she leveled at Phillip. She gave him a bright, wicked smile. "I'm Valentina Payton, Your Grace. And I'm here to kill you."

CHAPTER TWENTY-EIGHT

I n the darkness behind Phillip, Sophie was shaking so badly she was certain all the room's occupants could hear her teeth chattering. She was cold. So cold. Her hands were numb, and her feet felt like anvils. She watched the scene unfolding in front of her as if it were a dream—no, a nightmare. Whatever it was, it was completely unbelievable. She wanted to wake up. Valentina, her *stepmother*, was standing in the light of the two lanterns, aiming a pistol squarely at Phillip's chest. How was this happening?

Valentina had always been rude, selfish, and condescending, but capable of *murder*? Sophie's mind refused to believe the truth, even though it was standing in front of her wearing a purple gown and holding a pistol.

She'd suspected Valentina had known *something*, of course. Sophie had even considered that Valentina knew Malcolm had been murdered, but seeing her with an actual weapon and hearing her say she intended to *kill* Phillip... When had the entire world gone mad? Valentina, apparently, *was a murderer. Oh, God. What if Papa...?* No. There was no way Papa knew about this. No way Papa had anything to do with this. This was Valentina's doing alone. Her father might be a weak fool, but he was no killer.

More footsteps on the stairs sounded and Sophie watched in horror as the two men who'd brought them here dragged a kicking, fighting Lord Bellingham down the stairs. The marquess's ankles and wrists were shackled, but he still managed to get a few good licks in on his captors.

Valentina moved to the side to allow room for the trio. She spun her pistol toward Lord Bellingham. She shook her head and glared angrily at Hugh and Hillsdale. "You dolts. You should have sent for me the first night. You're both too timid to do what you must. If you want something done right, send a woman to do it. Just like when I had to take care of Malcolm."

Sophie had to bite her cheek to keep from gasping and making noise. *Valentina had killed Malcolm too?*

Valentina turned to Phillip. "Now. I'm going to kill you and your friend here, the marquess. Then I'm going to put the pistol in his hand to make it look as if he did it. And then Hillsdale's doctor will come and declare this a horrible falling out between two friends." She laughed a humorless laugh. "No offense, Lord Bellingham, but we'll also tell everyone that you killed Malcolm as well. You're a spy. You must have your reasons. Perhaps the good brothers were up to something nefarious. Only Phillip here must have got off one excellent shot before you killed him. *Such* a shame."

Sophie's shaking intensified. Her heart raced so quickly she couldn't breathe. This had to be what it felt like just before one fainted. Surely, she was about to. But she shook her head and forced herself to breathe more slowly. She'd never been a fainter, and she did not intend to become one now. She *could not* fail Phillip and Lord Bellingham. Not when her own evil stepmother was to blame for all of this.

Valentina had murdered Malcolm Grayson. And now she intended to kill both Phillip and the marquess.

Not while Sophie had breath in her body.

Valentina stepped forward. "Who's first?" she asked in a silky, calm purr. "I daresay the good *duke* should be the first to die! He's made me the angriest."

"Why's that?" Phillip asked quickly, clearly attempting to delay Valentina from her task.

Valentina's smirk widened. "Why, isn't it obvious, *Your Grace*? You've caused all this trouble. If you'd only died on the Continent like you should have, none of this would have happened."

"You killed Malcolm because you believed I was already dead?" Phillip asked, anger making his voice sharp. He was obviously trying to delay the inevitable.

"Yes," Valentina replied, giving Phillip her most charming catlike smile. "And it was all going quite well, too. We *had* the blasted title...until *you* resurrected yourself."

"My apologies for remaining alive," Phillip said with irony dripping from his voice. "But how exactly did *you* have Malcolm's title? It belonged to Hugh, didn't it?"

Valentina impatiently waved the pistol in the air. She gave Phillip a tight smile. "Hugh couldn't find his way out of an opened door. We tell him what to do, how to vote, and...who to marry." She slithered over to Lord Hillsdale and kissed him on the cheek. "Don't we, darling?"

"That's right, my love," Hillsdale replied, kissing Valentina fully on the lips.

Sophie nearly gagged. Valentina and Lord Hillsdale? Ugh. In addition to being a murderer, the woman was apparently a cheater, too.

"You do not!" Hugh insisted, stamping his foot.

"Shut up, you fool," Valentina shot back at him without even looking in his direction.

"Right, then," Hugh replied, hanging his head and kicking at the ground like an errant schoolboy. Sophie fought the urge to roll her eyes.

Valentina moved back over to stand in front of Phillip and waved the pistol in the air again. She jerked her chin toward Hugh. "If you hadn't fouled this up, I wouldn't have to do this."

"I don't know what you're talking about," Hugh replied, closing his eyes and turning away. "In fact, I was never here and I'm not here now. I know nothing about this. I'm going back to London immediately."

"That's a good idea," Valentina replied. "Go. We'll tell you what to do next when we get back."

Hugh wasted no time making his way up the stairs and out the door.

Sophie watched him go with disgust. It was just like that ninny to run away at a time like this.

Standing only a few lengths from Phillip, Valentina raised her arm and pointed the pistol at his chest. "Very well, dukes first." She cocked the hammer.

Just as Valentina pulled the trigger, Sophie launched herself from the darkness and flew between her stepmother and Phillip. "Nooooooo!" she screamed. A horrendous pain tore through her chest, and she fell to the ground in a heap in front of Phillip. The last thing she saw before her world went black was all the blood.

CHAPTER TWENTY-NINE

Phillip didn't think. He sprang into action, leaping at Valentina and tackling her, knocking the pistol out of her hand.

Bell quickly bent over and grabbed the pistol and broke off his shackles on his knee. Then he stuck his fingers in his mouth and made a loud whistling noise that pierced the air. Meanwhile, Phillip grabbed Hillsdale with an arm around the neck, the knife to his throat.

"Give me a reason to kill you right now, please," Phillip growled into the older man's ear.

"Don't hurt me!" Hillsdale begged, quickly offering his pistol to Bell, who ripped it from his limp hand with obvious pleasure.

Bonham and the smaller man took off up the stairs, clearly trying to flee. But Phillip wasn't concerned with either of them at the moment. He shoved Hillsdale at Bell to guard before dropping to his knees at Sophie's side.

He'd cradled her head in his lap. She was unconscious, blood oozing from a hole in the upper right-side of her chest.

"No, Sophie. No. Don't go. Stay with me. Stay with me," he pleaded in a ragged voice.

Mrs. Jarvis was suddenly at his side, her hand on his shoulder. "I've sent for the doctor, Yer Grace."

"I had no idea she was here," Valentina said incredulously from the spot on the floor near the staircase where she'd remained cowering since Phillip tackled her. She was staring at Sophie. "What is she doing here?" Valentina yelled at Hillsdale.

Hillsdale winced and gulped.

Thunderous sets of footsteps sounded on the stairs as General Grimaldi came rushing down with a half a dozen men behind him.

Bell nodded toward Valentina. "There's the first piece of rubbish to take out."

Grimaldi himself pulled Valentina from the floor and shackled her. "I'll use real shackles this time," he said, winking at Bell.

"Your shackles were fake!" Valentina said accusingly to Bell.

"Of course they were," Bell said, bowing to the woman. "No self-respecting spy allows his *accoutrements* to be taken away without a purpose. By the by, why do they call you the Jackal?"

A vein throbbed in Valentina's neck and her face turned a mottled purple color. "What? The Jackal? *Who* called me a jackal?"

Hillsdale turned even paler while Valentina's eyes spit fire.

She continued to glare at them all as she was led upstairs by one of Grimaldi's men while Bell shrugged and said, "Well, *that* was awkward."

Phillip was vaguely aware of Grimaldi telling Bell, "We've already got the two men who tried to run away...and Hugh

Grayson. That fool trotted out several minutes ago and sat inside a carriage, apparently waiting for someone to drive him back to London."

The rest was all a haze to Phillip, who just kept repeating over and over. "Don't leave me. Don't leave me," as he cradled Sophie in his arms. He paused long enough to issue orders to Mrs. Jarvis. "Bring blankets. Get the maids to make up the bedchamber at the top of the stairs. The nicest one. We'll need sheets and hot water and bandages," he said, trying to recall all the things they'd used on him when he'd finally been dragged into the surgeon's tent off the battlefield.

"I'm carrying her upstairs myself!" Phillip insisted when Bell attempted to ask Mrs. Jarvis to call for footmen to move Sophie from the cellar floor. Phillip gathered Sophie in his arms and lifted her as gently as possible. She had been unconscious since she'd fallen, but he'd kept his fingers on the pulse in her neck and knew she was still alive. His jaw tight, his head filled with one prayer, he carried Sophie's limp body up the cellar stairs, through the kitchens, through the corridors, across the foyer and up the wide, winding marble staircase to the guest chamber that had already been prepared for her.

Phillip gently laid her on the bed and fell to his knees. It felt as if an eternity had passed before the doctor from the nearby village arrived.

"Do you have laudanum?" Phillip asked, jumping to his feet as the doctor hurried into the bedchamber.

"Yes," the doctor replied.

"Lots of it?" Phillip prodded. He recalled only too well the ungodly pain he'd experienced when they'd taken the ball from his shoulder. The doctor would probably have to do the same with Sophie.

"Indeed, Your Grace," the doctor replied. He wasted no time opening the bag he'd brought with him and setting it on the bed next to Sophie. "Rip open her gown. I must see the wound," he ordered the two housemaids who stood at the ready to help him.

Bell and Grimaldi chose that moment to step forward and place a hand on Phillip's shoulders. The two men stood on either side of him.

"Come away," Bell said quietly but firmly. "You can do no more for her here."

"Absolutely not," Phillip replied. He made to push off their hands, but the two men exchanged a look and a nod before grabbing Phillip securely by the arms.

Phillip fought Bell and Grimaldi like a wild dog, making them struggle to drag him from the room.

"You must allow the doctor and the maids to care for her in private," Bell said, cursing under his breath as he tried to reason with Phillip.

In the end, they had to enlist two of Grimaldi's men to help pull Phillip away, down to the study, where Grimaldi poured him a towering glass of brandy. "Drink this, Harlowe. And don't say another bloody word until that glass is empty."

Phillip begrudgingly complied.

CHAPTER THIRTY

hillip couldn't pace any longer. He'd spent the last six days walking back and forth outside the door to Sophie's sick room while the doctors came in and out at all hours examining her. When he wasn't pacing, he was at her side, easing her fever with a cold rag on her forehead, dripping bits of ice into her slack mouth, or holding her hand and praying to whatever God would listen to make her well again.

He stopped pacing and slowly lowered himself into the chair that Bell had insisted the footmen bring up in case Phillip finally passed out. It just might happen. He hadn't eaten. He hadn't slept. The nightmares were back. Only this time they involved Sophie's body lying crumpled on the floor of the cellar, blood seeping from a shot wound on her chest.

Phillip had tried to cry, but the tears wouldn't come. Instead, he'd railed. He'd shouted. He'd even bargained with God. But every time a maid or doctor came out of Sophie's bedchamber, their faces were drawn and pale. They shook their heads at him and said entirely unhelpful things like, "It's grave. Quite grave, indeed."

Phillip was tired of hearing that word. Only he truly dreaded another word that would be much worse.

Dead.

She's dead.

He wouldn't be able to stand it if *those* words were uttered. Those words would break him. He laid his head back against the wall behind him and shut his eyes for the first time in days.

But he couldn't sleep. He couldn't cry. He had promised Sophie no harm would come to her. He was a damned liar and if she died, he'd never forgive himself. He wouldn't deserve forgiveness.

One of their conversations haunted him. She had wanted to leave the cellar. She'd asked him to fetch the constable instead of waiting for Hugh to return. And Phillip had refused her. He'd been so convinced he could keep her safe. Her injury was his fault, and her death would be too.

Boots sounded on the marble steps coming up the grand staircase. When the footsteps stopped, Phillip opened his eyes to see Bell and Dr. Morrison from London standing in front of him. The good doctor was one of many of London's finest Phillip had insisted come to give their opinion of Sophie's condition.

"I'm going in to check on her," Dr. Morrison declared, lifting his chin toward Sophie's room.

Phillip nodded once, and the doctor disappeared into the bedchamber, while Phillip eyed the marquess through eyes he knew were bloodshot.

Bell had a recalcitrant look on his face. A look rarely attributed to the spy.

"Have you seen her today?" Bell asked quietly. He stood at attention with his back ramrod straight as if he believed the more formal he made things, the less the truth would hurt.

"Same as yesterday," Phillip murmured. He was so tired.

So tired he could barely think. But he didn't dare sleep. If he was asleep when Sophie… No. He couldn't even contemplate it.

"At least she's no worse," Bell offered, clearing his throat uncomfortably.

"Don't." The word was a command, not a request.

Bell scratched at the back of his neck. "Harlowe, I—"

"Do you trust her *now*?" Phillip managed through his dry, cracked lips. "After she risked her life for me?"

"You know I do," Bell replied, his hands folded in front of him. He cleared his throat again and stared at the floor. They'd already had this talk. The first night. After Phillip had finished his glass of brandy. He'd yelled at Bell until his lungs had nearly given out. And Bell had let him do it. Somehow sensing that Phillip needed it. He needed to let out all the grief and anger and sadness he'd been feeling for so long. But nothing had been resolved that night. Phillip had left the room in disgust, hurrying up to begin his vigil outside Sophie's bedchamber.

"I doubted her, Bell." Phillip shook his head and leaned forward, staring unseeing at his boots and the parquet floor. He clasped his hands in front of him. "For a moment, when we were first abducted, I doubted her. For a half a second, I thought she might have told them where I would be."

"How were you to know—?"

"Do you know *why* I doubted her?" Phillip asked, his voice still hoarse.

Bell lifted his chin and briefly closed his eyes. "Because I led you to believe she was guilty," he said in a gruff, regretful voice.

Phillip rested his elbows on his knees and let his head drop into his hands. "Do you know how badly I want to blame you?" He turned his head slowly and stared at his friend. "But I can't. I'm the one who knew her. Not you. I did this to her, Bell. This is my fault. No one else is to blame."

Bell walked over and placed a hand on Phillip's shoulder. "Miss Payton is one of the bravest souls I've ever met," the marquess said quietly. "I've known grown men, trained spies, who wouldn't have done what she did."

Phillip closed his eyes and heaved a heavy sigh. "If I lose her, Bell. If she—"

"Gentlemen," came Dr. Morrison's steady voice from the bedchamber doorway.

Phillip's eyes shot open. He nearly jumped from the chair.

"How is she, doctor?" Bell asked, quietly.

The doctor shook his head, his face drawn and pale. "It's dire, Your Grace. Quite dire, indeed."

Phillip turned, and cursing under his breath, slammed his fist into the wall.

CHAPTER THIRTY-ONE

Sophie slowly became aware of light behind her eyelids. She sluggishly lifted them and blinked. Pain shot through her entire body. Turning her head took effort, but she managed to move it to take in her surroundings. She was in a bed. A lovely, comfortable bed that wasn't her own. In a lovely, comfortable bedchamber that also wasn't her own. Daylight streamed in through the nearby windows, and the scent of lilies and lemon wax filled the air.

A movement to her right caught her attention and, with effort, she turned her head to see…her father. He was sitting in a chair next to her bed, his head slumped to his shoulder in sleep.

It all came flooding back to her. The kidnapping, the captivity, her time in the cellar with Phillip, and the fact that…she'd been shot. That's why her body ached. And that's why she was in bed right now. She must still be at Phillip's estate.

"Papa." She tried to speak, but her throat was dry and the sound that came from her cracked lips was more like a grunt than a word.

Papa started. His dark hair was mussed, there were large, dark circles beneath his eyes. He was unshaved, his clothes were rumpled, and his cravat untied. He blinked and looked around, obviously reorienting himself before seeing her. "Sophia!" he nearly shouted.

"Papa," she tried again, but the result wasn't much better. This time, it sounded like a croak.

"You're awake." His voice was quieter, but she could still hear the surprise in it. He was frantically searching her face.

"Water...water?" she rasped, able to utter only that single word.

Her father stood and hurried to the sideboard, where a pitcher of water and a glass were at the ready. He poured so quickly that he spilled the water. But he grabbed the glass and made his way back to the bedside immediately.

He placed the glass beneath her lips and lifted it so she could drink. She gulped down two large sips—breathing heavily from the exertion—before sitting back against the pillows that Papa was already propping behind her.

"How long was I asleep?" she finally asked after wincing and adjusting her position a bit.

"Eight...it's been eight days," he told her, searching her face again. The look of relief on his features worried her. Exactly how serious had the situation been?

"I assume I'm...that this is...I'm still at...the duke's estate?" she asked, biting her lip.

"Yes." Papa said, frowning. "This is one of the guest rooms."

"What did the doctor say?" she asked next, wondering where Phillip was.

"He... He..." Papa swallowed and shook his head.

Was she imagining it, or were tears coming from the corners of his eyes? She'd never seen her father cry before.

Not even when Mama died. "Papa?" She could hear the panic in her own voice.

"Sophia," he began again, scrubbing his face with his hand, "he told me you probably wouldn't wake up."

"What?" The breath left her body as if it had been stolen. That was why Papa had been watching her so closely, examining her so carefully. She sucked air through her nostrils and took three deep breaths. She'd been expected to die. Well, it felt to her as if she was very much alive.

"Was anyone else injured?" she asked, suddenly afraid that perhaps Phillip had been shot too.

"No. No one else was hurt."

Sophie frowned. "Where is Phil...ah, His Grace?"

"Off riding for all I know," Papa replied with a look of disgust on his face.

Sophie frowned, but decided to let the matter rest for the moment. "Have you been...sitting here this entire time?" she ventured.

"Mostly," Papa replied. "I didn't get word for at first. I came as soon as I was able."

Sophie glanced down at her body. "What...what exactly happened to me?"

"You were shot in the chest," Papa continued, his eyes filling with tears again.

Sophie nodded. She remembered being shot. It was everything afterward that remained hazy. "That explains why it feels as if I was run over by a carriage."

Papa pulled his chair closer to the bedside. He covered her closest hand with one of his. "You've had the finest surgeon from London. Dr. Morrison removed the ball and the bits of clothing from your wound."

The hint of a smile touched her lips. "That sounds... awful. I'm certainly glad I wasn't awake for that."

Papa squeezed her hand and managed a weak smile.

"What happened?" she asked, moving slightly and wincing again. "After I was shot, I mean. Was Valentina arrested?"

Papa nodded. "She was, and so were all the men with her, including Hugh Grayson."

Sophie bit her lip. Not entirely certain how much her father knew. "I heard her say she killed Malcolm, too."

Papa rubbed his jaw with his free hand and shook his head. The disgusted look had returned to his face. "Yes, well, General Grimaldi told me even more about Valentina's involvement."

"What did he say?" Sophie asked, half afraid to hear it.

Papa heaved another sigh. "Apparently, before we married, Valentina was after Malcolm Grayson. She wanted to marry him."

Sophie gasped. "I didn't know that. That was before my come-out. But it stands to reason. She's always been obsessed with being a duchess."

"She never mentioned it to me, either, of course," Papa added, a disgruntled look on his face.

"So Valentina had a reason to hate Malcolm?" Sophie said, still contemplating her stepmother's role in the whole sordid affair.

Papa nodded. "Apparently, she had vowed to connect herself to the Duke of Harlowe one way or another, and once the rumor circulated that Phillip Grayson had died at war, Valentina came up with the idea to murder Malcolm, replace him with Hugh, and convince Hugh to marry you. She knew Hugh was the sort she could bend to her will. Apparently, she'd met him once when he'd come to London asking for a handout from Malcolm. She and Hillsdale went to visit Hugh in the country after hearing the news of Phillip's death."

Sophie expelled her breath. "That's madness."

Papa shook his head. "I quite agree, but the most insane

part is that it nearly worked. If Phillip had truly been dead, she might well have got away with all of it."

"What did Hillsdale have to do with it?" Sophie asked, wondering if her father knew the extent of Valentina's betrayal.

Papa heaved a sigh. "Seems he was just a means to an end for Valentina. She began an affair with him to use him to help her execute her elaborate scheme."

Sophie squeezed her father's hand. "I'm sorry, Papa. It must have been quite painful for you to find out how awful she truly was."

Papa sighed again and stared at the floor. "No, Sophia. I'm the one who's sorry. After your mother's death, I spent too long in the country. I didn't come back to Society until you were of age. I never heard the rumors about Valentina. Apparently, Malcolm Grayson had bedded her but refused to court her. She was a young widow back then. Her first husband, Viscount Greenling, died under mysterious circumstances as well, I'm told." Papa shook his head.

Sophie gasped. "No!"

"Yes." Papa nodded. "For all I know, I may have been next."

Sophie shuddered. "Don't say that."

"Not to mention, she brought that hideous Hugh into our lives," Papa continued, his face turning red with anger. "I never did like him much. But Valentina convinced me a duke was the best possible match. And after your mother died, I always wanted the best for you. You deserved a duke, as far as I'm concerned. I let my common sense be overrun by my pride. I'm sorry, Sophia."

Sophia reached out and patted her father's hand. "I'm only glad I won't have to marry him after all, Papa."

"No," Papa agreed. "You won't. The blackguard is in gaol."

Sophie nodded. "Did General Grimaldi say whether Hugh was involved in Malcolm's murder?"

Papa shrugged. "General Grimaldi is still investigating, but from what he told me, Hugh was probably just a pawn used by Valentina and Lord Hillsdale to get what they wanted. Hugh was little more than oaf from the country who would do what they said in exchange for them taking him under his wing in London Society and puffing up his self-importance. Hugh was so arrogant and power-obsessed, he pretended not to notice their methods."

"Which would explain why Valentina didn't kill you to marry Hugh herself," Sophie pointed out.

Papa narrowed his eyes. "Honestly, I don't think she wanted him. Even if it would have made her a duchess. Though I suspect she probably considered it. Perhaps she thought it would be a bit too much of a coincidence if her *second* husband died early, too."

Sophie shuddered again. "I don't even want to think about that. Did General Grimaldi mention anything about Lord Vining? Did he have anything to do with it?"

Papa lifted his brows. "Vining, yes. Apparently, Hillsdale blackmailed Vining to help him cover up what truly happened to Malcolm. Hillsdale didn't want to get his own hands dirty, so he employed that lackwit Vining to go around bribing doctors and ensuring the right story got into the papers. Vining is in gaol now, too."

"Good," Sophie replied. She bit her lip before tentatively asking, "Did General Grimaldi tell you how Malcolm died?"

Papa shuddered, too. "Apparently, Valentina stabbed him in the back. No doubt he allowed her in, thinking of her only as a former lover. It makes sense. Lord Bellingham said the valet mentioned that a woman with dark hair wearing a green cape was seen sneaking down the back staircase the night Malcom Grayson was murdered."

"Oh, my goodness." Sophie's mouth fell open. "Valentina gave me that cape. She told me it looked good on me. I was suspicious at the time. Now I know why."

Papa's nostrils flared with anger. "I'm quite certain she would have been only too happy to blame you if she'd thought you were close to discovering the truth."

"It's all quite unbelievable," Sophie replied, shaking her head.

"Yes. And I'm an old fool." Papa took a deep breath. "I owe you an apology for bringing Valentina into our lives. I nearly ruined your life pairing you with Hugh. Not to mention, I could have lost you." Papa pulled his handkerchief from his coat pocket with his free hand and dabbed at his eyes.

Sophie pulled her hand from his and patted the top of it. "Thank you for apologizing, Papa," she said, tears burning her eyes too. "It means a great deal to me."

Papa continued to dab at his wet eyes. "I love you, Sophia, and I *won't* do wrong by you again. As soon as you're strong enough, I'm taking you away from here. We'll go to our country estate, where you can recuperate away from this awful family."

Sophie frowned. "Awful family?"

"The Graysons. Malcolm may have been innocent. But Hugh was a horror and Phillip nearly got you killed taking a bullet meant for him. I'm not about to allow any of them to hurt you *ever again*."

CHAPTER THIRTY-TWO

Phillip was sitting in his study the next day, staring morosely into a bottle of brandy as he drank his third glass of the stuff. Sophie had gone home this morning. She hadn't even said goodbye, not that Phillip could blame her. He didn't deserve her consideration. He'd nearly got her killed.

He'd tried to see her, of course. Every day after her father had arrived, he'd hovered outside her bedchamber door, waiting for Sir Roger to give him permission to enter. But that man had made it quite clear from the moment he'd stepped foot in the house that no one was to see Sophie without his express permission—and that permission certainly did not extend to Phillip.

He wouldn't even speak to Phillip. Instead, Sir Roger insisted upon hearing the story of what had transpired directly from General Grimaldi, who had obviously shared the fact that Valentina had been trying to shoot *Phillip* when Sophie had jumped in front of the pistol.

With every look, Sir Roger made it clearer that he had absolutely no use for Phillip. And Phillip couldn't blame him either. Phillip was paying the doctors, however, so he was at least aware of Sophie's progress. According to Dr. Morrison, she was healing nicely, and all hints of infection had gone. Her fever had broken, and Sophie was officially on the mend.

Phillip had never experienced such overwhelming relief. Not even when his speech had returned in Devon. But a sennight after her father arrived, she was gone.

He'd had words with Sir Roger, of course, before the man left. He'd asked one last time to visit Sophie, to say goodbye, and had once again been denied. "Sophia doesn't want to see you, Your Grace," Sir Roger had finally told him. "She's never asked for you. She wants to leave immediately."

Those words had felt like daggers in Phillip's heart, but no matter how painful it was, he would respect Sophie's wishes. She obviously blamed him for her condition, and she had every right to. There had been no promises between them. No plans for the future. They may have spent one heavenly night in each other's arms, but he'd been an arse and told her he would not promise her more. What else was she left to think? No. Phillip didn't blame Sophie for never wanting to see him again. He blamed himself.

A soft knock was followed by the study door cracking open and Bell sticking in his head.

"Looking for company?" Bell asked.

"No," Phillip growled. "I want to be alone right now. Besides, I thought you went back to London with Grim."

"I wanted to talk to you," Bell replied.

"Go away," Phillip growled again.

"I'll take that as a welcome. It's as good as I'm likely to get," Bell said with a grin, pushing open the door and coming to sit on the opposite side of Phillip's desk.

"Don't you dare tell me not to drink," Phillip told him, pouring himself more brandy.

"I wouldn't dream of it," Bell replied.

Phillip sighed and ran a hand through his hair. "Fine. Then you may stay." At least Bell could distract him from his thoughts of Sophie. "Any news of the prisoners?"

"Yes. They're all in gaol. Hillsdale, Valentina, and Vining are in the Tower, and Hugh and the other two men are in Newgate."

"Ah, Hugh's not in the Tower because he is no longer a duke," Phillip said with a smirk.

"That's right," Bell confirmed. "Though as the grandson of a duke, believe me, he was sorely put out to discover his fate."

"What *is* their fate?" Phillip asked, bringing the glass to his lips again.

"They must go before the judge, of course, but with the evidence we have against them, I'm certain Hillsdale and Valentina will be sentenced to death."

"And Vining?"

"He'll probably escape with his life. If he's lucky."

Phillip nodded grimly. "What about Sir Roger? Did he have anything to do with Malcolm's death?" he asked, half hoping Sophie's father would be carted off to gaol too.

Bell shook his head. "Absolutely nothing, as far as we could determine. Seems the poor old man was taken in by Valentina's looks after she'd been widowed and tossed over by most others. We're still looking into her first husband's death. She had a sullied reputation, and she used Sir Roger for his money, all the while plotting to align their family with the Harlowe name and taking up with Hillsdale and any other man who bought her expensive gifts, and did her bidding."

Phillip's nostrils flared. Valentina was obviously a monster. It made him ill to think of how long Sophie had been exposed to that villainous woman. "And Hugh? Did he plot to kill Malcolm, too?"

"We have yet to determine precisely how Hugh was

involved. He swears Malcolm was already dead when Hillsdale and Valentina arrived on his doorstep volunteering to help him navigate London Society and Parliament."

Phillip lifted his brows. "In exchange for?"

"Hugh's votes, of course. Hillsdale wanted a lackey who would do his bidding in Parliament, and Valentina wanted a duke in the family...for her stepdaughter. I hate to say it, but I tend to believe Hugh. He seems too dull to have been a part of it. Though I've no doubt he knew about it after the fact."

"I agree. He knew about it and was there at the end," Phillip said, examining the liquid in his glass while pictured himself punching his cousin in the gut. He really should have done it while he'd had the chance.

"Yes, and he'll be punished for his role in your abduction. Make no mistake." Bell plucked at his lip.

"I'm glad to hear it. What about Dr. Kilgore?"

"Dr. Kilgore agreed to tell the truth about what he saw the night Malcolm was killed. The papers have already caught wind of it. I'm afraid the whole messy tale will be in tomorrow's *Times*."

"Good," Phillip replied, tossing back the rest of the brandy. "That's what I wanted. The truth about what happened to Malcolm for all the town to know. He was a good brother and a fine duke. He deserved better." Phillip pushed the bottle away. "Thank you for helping me learn the truth, Bell."

"I was just doing my job," Bell said, shaking his head. "But I am sorry, Harlowe. I was wrong about Sophie."

A few moments of uncomfortable silence passed between them.

"How is Sophie?" Bell finally ventured.

"She's better." Phillip blew out his breath. "And she's gone."

Bell frowned. "Gone? What do you mean, gone?"

"She left with her father earlier. She didn't say goodbye."

"What?" Bell's frown intensified.

Phillip shook his head. His throat ached. "I don't blame Sophie for being unable to forgive me. I should have kept her safe."

Bell shook his head. "I understand how you feel, Harlowe. I do. It's just... Damn it. It's unfair."

The hint of a smile lifted Phillip's lips. "Life isn't fair, Bell. You of all people should know that."

"I do know that," Bell said with a shrug. "But I'm not used to unhappy endings."

Phillip sighed. "Yes, well. This one wasn't meant to be, I suppose."

"I simply cannot allow—"

"No, Bell, no," Phillip raised his voice. "I demand that you do *not* go speak to Sophie. Thea told me you're famous for trying to talk people into seeing things differently. That will not work this time. Sophie barely knows you and she doesn't particularly like you. She won't welcome a visit from you."

Bell expelled his breath and settled back into his chair. "I know that." He sighed. "I'm not a *complete* fool."

"Good. That's an end to it," Phillip declared, slapping a palm against the table.

"Well," Bell replied, cocking his head to the side. "It's not exactly an *end* to it."

Phillip narrowed his eyes at his friend. "What do you mean? You will not visit her, will you?"

"Certainly not," Bell replied, straightening his cravat. "I intend to send someone much more effective in my stead."

CHAPTER THIRTY-THREE

A fortnight later, Sir Roger Payton's town house in London

Sophie stepped into the corridor, shutting her father's study door behind her. She'd just finished informing Papa of her plans. It had really been much easier than she'd guessed it would be...telling her father precisely what she intended to do and gaining his approval. She was through with taking orders from men, and she was especially through with anyone else controlling her choices or her destiny. And most importantly, she would never settle for not being put *first* in someone's life ever again. And that included her father.

She'd had a great deal of time to think over the last two weeks. Being mostly bedridden gave one an awful lot of time to think, in fact. At first, she'd been dismayed that Phillip had never even tried to say goodbye to her. Papa had informed her that Phillip had shown no interest in either visiting her or saying goodbye. So be it. She needed to close that door behind her and move on in her life.

Obviously, after everything they'd been through, she and

Phillip Grayson hadn't been meant to be together. And after the debacle with Hugh, she was no longer interested in looking for another man to marry, either. A love like she'd had with Phillip was once in a lifetime. She planned to go to her father's country estate and live out her days in the small cottage there. She and Mary, her lady's maid, would be leaving first thing in the morning. Papa had agreed nearly immediately. His guilt over bringing Valentina into their lives remained almost palpable. She no longer blamed her father for his mistakes, however. She'd made mistakes too. But she wanted to get away from London, where the headlines included her name nearly every day. The country would be a welcome relief, even if it might become…lonely.

Sophie strolled through the corridor toward the staircase in the foyer, her head held high. She had physically healed from her injuries incurred in the cellar. Her heart might still be fragile, but she refused to allow anything to stop her now. The rest of her life was her own, and she intended to enjoy every moment. On her terms. She was choosing to be happy once and for all.

The new butler, the one she'd hired last week after tossing Roberts out on his ear without a reference, came hurrying toward her. "Miss Payton, I was just coming to inform you that you have a visitor."

Sophie stopped and frowned. A visitor? Who could it be? She hoped it wasn't General Grimaldi again. She'd already informed the insistent man that she had no intention of becoming a spy for the Home Office, even if she had displayed what he called 'a knack for subterfuge and uncommon bravery.' As far as she was concerned, she wasn't brave at all. She'd done precisely what she'd had to do to keep her stepmother from killing Phillip, the way the awful woman had killed his brother. But Sophie hardly relished a life filled with danger. On the contrary, she intended to do precisely what she'd informed Papa. She would live a quiet life in the countryside as a spinster.

"Here is her card," the butler replied, handing the small piece of vellum to Sophie.

Her? Sophie took the card and glanced at it. *Lady Theodora Clayton.* Oh. No. What could *she* possibly want? The last time they'd spoken had been beyond unpleasant.

"Tell her I'm not home," she informed the butler.

A soft clearing of the throat caught her attention and Sophie glanced toward the door of the nearby salon to see Lady Clayton standing in the entrance, staring at her. The woman was wearing a bright yellow gown with a matching redingote. Her gray eyes had a smile in them, and her dark hair was piled atop her head, held in place by a matching yellow bow. "I do hope you'll reconsider taking my call, Miss Payton," Lady Clayton said with a sardonic edge to her voice.

Drat. Sophie sighed. She couldn't lie to the woman directly to her face. Very well. But she'd simply ensure this visit was over quickly.

Nodding to the butler, Sophie made her way to the salon door and ushered Lady Clayton back inside before joining her and closing the door behind them.

Sophie remained standing, her arms folded across her chest. "You'll forgive me if I don't offer you a seat." Lady Clayton couldn't possibly believe her visit was welcome. Phillip had to have informed her somehow of what had transpired between them in the countryside. Why else would she be here?

"And you'll forgive me if I take one, regardless?" Lady Clayton said smoothly, taking a seat on the cream-colored settee in the center of the room.

Sophie sighed again. "What do you want, Lady Clayton? I fear I'm fresh out of the ability to mimic niceties this morning."

"I knew I liked you," Lady Clayton replied, the hint of a smile quirking up the corners of her mouth.

Sophie's only response was an arched brow.

"Very well," Lady Clayton continued. "I'm here on behalf of Phillip."

Sophie resisted the urge to roll her eyes. "Allow me to spare you wasting your time, Lady Clayton."

"Please, do call me Thea," the viscountess said, a perfectly pleasant smile on her face.

"Fine. *Thea*," Sophie replied somewhat impatiently. "What's happened between Phillip and me is private. I *know* you understand that. And I have no intention of discussing it with you or anyone else. Now, if you'll excuse me—"

"I do hope you'll do me the courtesy of at least *listening* to what I have to say," Thea said, calmly smoothing her skirts. "Phillip didn't ask me to come. In fact, he doesn't know I'm here."

"So, you're *not* here on his behalf?" Sophie replied, her brow furrowed.

"I'm not here at his *request*," Thea clarified. "I am here on his *behalf*."

Good heavens. The woman was speaking in riddles. "I fear I'm not following," Sophie replied. She had no time to play Lady Clayton's word games.

The viscountess lifted her chin, her hands now folded primly in her lap. "Allow me to be direct. As I recall, you appreciate directness."

At Sophie's nod, Thea continued. "Phillip is a mess, from what I understand. He's heartbroken. He's alone. And he knows well that he made an awful mistake in not telling you he was alive, and placing you in such danger at Graystone Manor."

Sophie's nostrils flared, and she kept her lips tightly closed. She gave Thea a tight smile. "You're wrong, Thea. If

Phillip wanted to apologize, he had ample time while I was recuperating at his estate. Now, I'll see you to the door."

"*I* must apologize as well," Thea continued, completely ignoring Sophie's second attempt to get rid of her. "I, too, made a mistake when you came to visit me. I should have told you more. I had a good feeling about you then, but I allowed my loyalty to Phillip to keep me from providing you with information you clearly needed to know."

Sophie paused. Blast it. The woman had piqued her curiosity. She turned back to face the viscountess. "What information?" Sophie ventured, arms still crossed over her chest.

"The truth about Phillip," Thea said softly.

"What do you mean?" Sophie took a few steps toward Thea, narrowing her eyes on the viscountess.

Thea cleared her throat and lifted her chin. "May I tell you a story, Miss Payton?"

Oh, heavens. Not a story. Sophie eyed Thea carefully. "It is a heart-warming one?"

"Indubitably."

Sophie bit her lip. "Will it stir and affect me?"

"I hope so," Thea replied with a smile.

"Very well." Sophie marched over and reluctantly lowered herself into the blue velvet-covered chair across from the viscountess. "Tell me the story," she said with a nod. "And you may as well call me Sophie."

Thea took a deep breath and settled her skirts before meeting Sophie's gaze again. "I met my husband by sneaking into his stables and breaking my leg," she began.

"What?" Sophie asked, blinking. She wasn't entirely certain she'd heard the viscountess correctly. "Why did you sneak into his stables?"

Thea cocked her head to the side. "I wanted to visit the horse he'd recently purchased at auction. Phillip's horse."

"Alabaster?" Sophie breathed.

"Yes, Alabaster," Thea replied, a lovely smile gracing her lips as she uttered the horse's name.

"Phillip often mentioned Alabaster when he wrote me from the Continent," Sophie added.

"Yes. Phillip adores Alabaster, as you know. What *my husband* didn't know was that I did, too. Alabaster was *my* horse when he was a foal. So I was sneaking around Ewan's stables to visit Alabaster."

"Why didn't you simply ask Lord Clayton if you could visit Alabaster?" Sophie asked, blinking again.

Thea pursed her lips to the side and tapped her chin. "Hmm. I believe I shall refrain from sharing that part of the story because the answer does not paint me or my character in an appealing light."

Sophie couldn't stifle her laugh.

Thea continued, "Suffice it to say that while sneaking about the stables, I broke my leg and was forced to remain at Ewan's estate until my leg healed."

"And Phillip was staying there also at that time?" Sophie prompted.

"Precisely," Thea replied. "Phillip was there, though I didn't know it at first. Eventually Ewan asked me to speak to him."

Sophie's brow remained furrowed. "What do you mean? Didn't you see each other at dinner?"

"No." Thea shook her head. "Phillip didn't come to dinner. Because…" Thea's gaze locked with Sophie's. "Phillip didn't speak."

Sophie swallowed and blew out her breath slowly. "I know. Phillip told me."

"But did he tell you how bad it was?" Thea asked, a warning note in her tone.

Sophie narrowed her eyes. "What do you mean?"

"I mean, by the time I met Phillip, he hadn't said a word in *months*," Thea continued.

"How many months?" Sophie ventured, her heart pounding.

"Six," Thea replied.

Sophie gasped. It felt as if someone had knocked the wind from her lungs. "Six?" she replied, her eyes filling with tears despite herself. She couldn't help but think that all those months she'd believed he was dead, Phillip had been struggling to speak. It must have been excruciating for him. He hadn't wanted her to see him like that, hadn't wanted to hold her to their promised engagement if he could not speak ever again.

"Ewan was at his wits' end," Thea continued. "He had tried everything, including purchasing Alabaster."

"When...when did Phillip begin to speak again?" Sophie ventured.

"I visited him every day for weeks," Thea replied. "And it wasn't until I mentioned Alabaster that he finally said something...the horse's name."

The tears that had filled Sophie's eyes slowly slid down her cheeks. She didn't want to know this. She didn't want to hear this story. She dashed away the tears with both hands. "With all due respect, Thea. I'm uncertain what this has to do with my relationship with Phillip," she said as she struggled to keep her breathing even.

Thea leaned forward and put her hands in her lap, watching Sophie's face. "The fact is that Phillip was devastated after the war. He nearly died on that battlefield."

Sophie nodded. "I know. Phillip never wanted to be a soldier, you know. He wanted to be a scholar. His father wouldn't allow it."

"I didn't know that," Thea said softly. "But it stands to

reason. He's a very kind man. One of the best I've ever known."

"I was so worried about him," Sophie continued, the memories sweeping her back to a time and place that she thought she'd buried in the past. "I prayed for him night and day...until my knees were scarred."

"You loved him very much," Thea said. "And he loved you. He told me about you...eventually, after he could speak again."

A lump formed in Sophie's throat. "He did?"

"Yes." Thea nodded. "He showed me your letter." Thea opened her reticule and pulled out a worn-looking folded piece of vellum. She offered it to Sophie.

Sophie's heart pounded. Trepidation spiked through her belly. She stared at the letter as if it were a viper. "Wha... what is that?"

"It's the letter Phillip wrote you from Devon. Lord Bellingham convinced him not to send it. It's been hidden in his rooms there ever since."

Sophie's throat closed. She couldn't breathe. She placed a hand at her throat. "Does he...know you have it?"

Thea shook her head. "No. But I daresay he would have wanted you to have it, eventually. Read it, Sophie. It's lovely."

Sophie forced herself to stand and step over to where Thea sat. Sophie's own hand shook as she took the letter from Thea's hand and walked swiftly over to the window where she unfolded it and read it through eyes blurred with tears.

My dearest S,
I write this letter with a hand that barely works, a ball hole
in my shoulder, and several broken ribs. I hate that it has to
be this way, but I want you to know that I am not dead.
Please tell no one. I may not come back to you in one piece.

I may not come back at all. I am in pieces at the moment.
Not the whole man you deserve. But know that I always
loved you and would have spent eternity loving you.
Forever,
P

Sophie lifted her head and stared unseeing out the window. "He told me he wrote me a letter. I didn't believe him."

"I understand," Thea said quietly. "Believe me, I do. Being in love can be frightening. It can cause the best of us to do frankly stupid things. I rejected Ewan at least twice before I accepted him."

Sophie frowned. "Why?"

"Because I couldn't believe that he could love me."

Sophie swung around to face Thea, wiping away her tears with her fingertips. "You rejected him?"

"Yes." Thea nodded. "And would you like to know what I learned?"

Sophie sighed. The hint of a smile touched her lips. "I have a feeling I don't have a choice."

Thea smiled. "I learned that sometimes, we hold on to pain on purpose. We *choose* to be martyrs. We choose to suffer."

Sophie lifted her chin. "I *choose* to be in control of my destiny. I'm going to live in the country."

"Is your destiny to be alone when you could have true love?" Thea countered.

Sophie let out a deep sigh. She clenched her jaw in frustration. "I don't...know any longer."

"Listen." Thea leaned toward Sophie. "You said Phillip never wanted to be a soldier. But he never wanted to be a man whose older brother was killed and left him with a dukedom and a murder mystery to solve, either. I know you're hurt. But believe me when I tell you that Phillip didn't know who he could trust when he came back to town. And it didn't help that you were betrothed to Hugh when he returned. Not that I'm blaming you, of course. I understand how powerful one's family's wishes can be. It's just that...the only people Phillip knew for certain he *could* trust were Ewan, Lord Bellingham, and myself. And Lord Bellingham, who is usually quite right about things, was awfully wrong about you. He told Phillip repeatedly that you may have been involved in Malcolm's death. He had Ewan and me half-convinced as well."

"You made that quite clear on our last visit." Sophie's nostrils flared.

"Yes, well. I am sorry. I was wrong. But every time Lord Bellingham told him to be wary of you, *Phillip* insisted you had nothing to do with it."

A lump lodged in Sophie's throat. "He did."

Thea nodded. "Yes. Without fail."

"Lord Bellingham is a horse's arse," Sophie said with a sniff.

Thea chuckled. "Lord Bellingham is my friend. I've spoken to him, and he asked me to tell you he's quite sorry that he tried to convince Phillip to mistrust you. Lord Bellingham wants you to know that even excellent spies sometimes make mistakes."

Sophie's face remained skeptical. Her arms remained crossed over her chest.

Thea gave her a tentative smile. "I must tell you, my friends and I...we're usually all quite a jolly, loyal lot when you get to know us. Please give us another chance...especially Phillip. He is ever so deserving of happiness, and I know he loves you desperately."

Sophie shook her head and closed her eyes. Why was Thea making her feel so...torn? So uncertain. She had her mind made up. She was ready to begin her life again, without Phillip in it. "If he loves me so desperately, why didn't he visit while I was recuperating at his house? Why didn't he even bother to say goodbye? I have no reason to believe he *wants* another chance."

Thea's brow knitted into a definitive frown. "What do you mean? He tried to visit. He tried to say goodbye."

This time, Sophie allowed herself to roll her eyes. "That's not true. My father told me Phillip never asked to visit."

Thea shook her head. "Phillip was at your bedside day and night until your father arrived at Graystone Manor. He sent for the best doctors in London to come to your side. He didn't sleep. According to Lord Bellingham, he was an unshaven, red-eyed wreck. He nursed you back to health and came away from your bedside only because your father ordered him out."

Sophie froze. Could what Lady Clayton said possibly be true? Or was she merely trying to convince Sophie of something that never happened to suit her own purposes? She narrowed her eyes at the viscountess. "Papa said he never came. And he never told me that *Phillip* was the one who sent for Dr. Morrison."

Thea folded her arms over her chest, a determined look in her eye. "Call your father in here now," she offered. "Let's ask him, shall we?"

CHAPTER THIRTY-FOUR

A sennight later, Graystone Manor

Phillip stood in the stables, stroking Alabaster's fine coat with a currycomb. He had stopped having the nightmares. The ones where screams and death met his ears. And the ones where Malcolm reached for him. Now his nightmares were of a different sort altogether. Sophie was there and when he reached for her, she disappeared. He frantically searched the darkness for her, but she was gone. He could never find her. He'd wake up in a sweat, panting, and filled with dread.

His nightmares had come true. Sophie was gone forever, and he had no one to blame but himself.

He might be alone, but he'd made one decision. From now on, for the rest of his life, his life was his own. And he would spend it living as he pleased. He may have lost Sophie, but he was no longer a soldier. He was free to visit faraway lands, to read as many books as he pleased, and to spend time with Alabaster, the horse who had survived the worst with him.

Footsteps sounded behind Phillip. But not the steady clomp of his stable master's boots. Blast. No doubt it was Bell coming to say more things Phillip didn't want to hear. "If you've come with more pithy anecdotes, Bellingham, save yourself the trouble."

"I quite agree. I've had my fill of pithy anecdotes as well."

His heart nearly stopping, Phillip swiveled to see Sophie standing several lengths away. She was wearing brown kid boots and a soft blue day dress with a wide white sash along the bodice and a matching bonnet with the same color ribbon. She had a smile on her face, and she looked more lovely than he'd ever seen her.

"Sophie," he breathed reverently, his heart still pounding.

Sophie strode toward him and stood next to him, then nodded toward the horse. "Well, aren't you going to introduce me?"

As if he understood the lady's request, Alabaster shook his mane while Phillip shook himself. "Oh, er, of course. This is Alabaster." He rubbed his hand down the horse's muzzle. "Alabaster. This is Miss Payton."

Sophie curtsied to the horse and smiled. "Oh, now. I don't think I should be so formal with your best friend," she said. "You may call me Sophie, Alabaster."

The horse whinnied and neighed as if he understood. He also stamped his hoof.

Sophie and Phillip both laughed, and Sophie reached out and stroked Alabaster on the nose. "You're a lovely boy, aren't you?"

"Don't tell him that," Phillip said, his mouth quirked up at the side. "He's already far too certain of himself by half. You'll make him arrogant."

"A boy this handsome *should* be arrogant," Sophie replied, scratching the horse behind his ears. "Funny, I always assumed he was white."

Phillip patted the horse's side. "No. Black as night. Always has been. Thea named him. She owned him when he was a foal. I believe she said she liked the irony."

"She told me," Sophie replied. "The part about owning him when he was a foal, at least. And about breaking her leg in Lord Clayton's stables."

"That's Thea for you." Phillip swallowed. He couldn't keep up the small talk any longer. It was killing him. "What are you doing here, Sophie?" He hoped his voice didn't sound as desperate to her as it did to him.

"I was on my way to Everly Hall," she replied, still directing her attention to Alabaster.

Phillip frowned. "Everly Hall is in Kent."

"I know. You didn't allow me to finish. I was on my way to Everly Hall when Lady Clayton came to visit me in London."

Phillip bowed his head and scuffed his boot in the dirt. "Oh."

"Do you know what she said to me?" Sophie continued.

Phillip lifted his head and scratched the back of his neck. "I can only imagine."

"She gave me this letter." Sophie pulled a piece of vellum from her reticule and showed it to him.

Phillip sighed. He knew it immediately. Leave it to Thea to get straight to the heart of the matter and show Sophie that damn letter. "And what did you respond?"

"I didn't," Sophie replied. "But I had a long time to think on my way to Everly Hall. A very long time."

"And?" he breathed. The letter didn't change the facts. The letter didn't turn back time. But Sophie was here, standing next to him. Talking to him. What had she thought when she read it?

Sophie shrugged. "In addition to this letter, Lady Clayton had quite a lot to say."

Phillip winced. "Such as?"

"Such as informing me that you nursed me back to health at Graystone Manor before Papa came and tried to visit every day after, but he wouldn't let you."

"He didn't tell you, did he?" Phillip asked, wincing yet again.

"No," Sophie replied. "He didn't. But he told the truth when Thea and I confronted him."

Phillip scratched the back of his neck. "Dare I asked what he said?"

"He said he didn't tell me because he was protecting me from you."

"I see."

A small smile perched on Sophie's lips. "He doesn't have a good opinion of your family."

Phillip rocked back and forth on his heels. "I cannot blame him."

"But then I pointed out that we've all made mistakes. His is named Valentina."

Relief swept through Phillip and a smile spread across his face. He stepped toward Sophie, intent on scooping her into his arms. "Does this mean—?"

She stopped him with a finger to the chest. "Not so fast. First, you must promise me you will always put me first, treasure me, and most importantly...*trust* me."

"Of course," he agreed.

"And second, my father asked me to insist you never put me in harm's way again."

"Never!" Phillip vowed.

Sophie continued to point her finger at him. "Third, I do *not* want a huge wedding. Huge weddings are far too formal. Everyone is on their best behavior. No one wears too many feathers to a huge wedding. They wear them to small weddings."

"We'll have the least formal wedding a duke and duchess ever had," he promised, nodding and laughing. "With all the feathers you'd like."

"*I* will not wear any, of course," Sophie replied, grinning back at him, "but I expect Lady Cranberry to do so. In fact, I may send her some."

"I'll write it on her invitation myself," Phillip vowed.

"Perfect." Sophie laughed before crossing her arms over her chest and lifting one brow. "I must say, your friends are quite insistent when they want to be. Apparently, Lord Bellingham is usually the one who delivers the speeches, but Thea was quite effective as well."

"Thea is a great friend," Phillip replied, making a mental note to buy Thea whatever she fancied the next time he saw her.

"Yes, she has vowed to be as loyal to me as she's been to you," Sophie continued. "She even volunteered to go to the Tower and visit Valentina with me before I left town."

Phillip's eyes flew open wide. "You visited Valentina?"

Smiling, Sophie reached out and petted Alabaster's nose again. "I couldn't resist. I took pleasure in informing her of what an idiot she is because the untitled man I was in love with—the one she told me to forget three years ago—is now the Duke of Harlowe."

Phillip threw back his head and laughed. "I would have loved to have seen her face when you told her that."

"You'll have to pay her a visit at the Tower next time you're in town," Sophie replied.

Phillip shook his head. "No. I don't care if I ever see her again. I intend to spend my days in the country from now on. Where there are no dramatics."

"I don't blame you." Sophie became quiet. "Phillip, I hope you realize that Malcolm's death had nothing to do with you. Valentina is insane. It was her choice to turn murderous."

Phillip expelled his breath. "I do know that now...because of you."

"You could even say it was my fault," Sophie continued. "If Valentina hadn't been so set on seeing me married to a duke, Malcolm might still be alive."

"No, Sophie. It's just as you said. Valentina is mad. And it was Malcolm's misfortune to have ever crossed paths with her. According to Bell, she was so obsessed with my brother, she might have still planned to murder both of us if I'd returned sooner."

"Valentina is where she belongs," Sophie replied.

"Sophie." Phillip stepped toward her and took her hand. He looked her in the eye. "I cannot promise you I won't ever go mute again."

Sophie nodded. "It makes perfect sense that you couldn't speak. Didn't you tell me you were found on the battlefield by two English soldiers?"

"Yes," Phillip answered.

"I'm certain you were terrified. You had to be entirely quiet—despite the ungodly amount of pain you were no doubt in—because the slightest noise might have given you away before you realized who the soldiers were. You could have been killed for making a noise, Phillip. No wonder you went mute."

Phillip closed his eyes and clasped Sophie's hands with his more tightly. "You're right, Sophie. I never thought of that."

"Don't you realize, Phillip? I understand. I've always understood. When I'm in a confined space, such as a carriage, my mind goes completely numb. I have no control over it. You've helped me time and time again, and if I need to, I'll help you. That's what love is."

Phillip stepped forward and pulled her into his arms in a tight embrace. "I love you so much, Sophie."

She hugged him back. "I love you, too, Phillip. I always have."

Phillip pulled away from her but kept her hands clasped in his. "There's one more thing I have to say. I didn't get the chance while you were so sick."

"What is it?" she prompted.

He squeezed her fingers. "Thank you for saving my life," he said solemnly.

"You know General Grimaldi offered me a position with the Home Office?" Sophie asked, smiling.

Phillip grinned. "And?"

"And I turned him down. Though I told Thea she should apply for the position. She's quite good. She would make an excellent negotiator with the French. As for me, I, too, intend to spend my days in the country from now on...here, if you'll have me."

"Have you?" Phillip took another step toward her and swung her up into his arms. "Of course, my love. We'll stay right here and have the most humdrum life a duke and duchess ever had. We get Alabaster half the time, you know? The other half of the year, he'll be in Devon with Clayton and Thea."

"Sounds lovely. I daresay we've had quite enough dramatics for one lifetime. For example, we're the only future duke and duchess I can think of who've *both* been shot."

Phillip tossed back his head and laughed. "That is true. But I daresay there will be *some* dramatics in our future. Not ours, of course—but just wait until you meet the rest of our friends."

∾

THANK YOU FOR READING. I hope you enjoyed Phillip's and Sophie's story. It is the last book in The Footmen's Club series. If you haven't read the others, CLICK HERE to read the first book, *The Footman and I.*

ALSO BY VALERIE BOWMAN

The Footmen's Club

The Footman and I (Book 1)

Duke Looks Like a Groomsman (Book 2)

The Valet Who Loved Me (Book 3)

Save a Horse, Ride a Viscount (Book 4)

Earl Lessons (Book 5)

The Duke is Back (Book 6)

Playful Brides

The Unexpected Duchess (Book 1)

The Accidental Countess (Book 2)

The Unlikely Lady (Book 3)

The Irresistible Rogue (Book 4)

The Unforgettable Hero (Book 4.5)

The Untamed Earl (Book 5)

The Legendary Lord (Book 6)

Never Trust a Pirate (Book 7)

The Right Kind of Rogue (Book 8)

A Duke Like No Other (Book 9)

Kiss Me At Christmas (Book 10)

Mr. Hunt, I Presume (Book 10.5)

No Other Duke But You (Book 11)

Secret Brides

Secrets of a Wedding Night (Book 1)

Thank you for reading *The Duke is Back*. It's been such fun to write the Footmen's Club series!

I'd love to keep in touch.

- Visit my website for information about upcoming books, excerpts, and to sign up for my email newsletter: www.ValerieBowmanBooks.com or at www.ValerieBowmanBooks.com/subscribe.
- Join me on Facebook: http://Facebook.com/ValerieBowmanAuthor.
- Reviews help other readers find books. I appreciate all reviews. Thank you so much for considering it!

Want to read the other Footmen's Club books?

- The Footman and I
- Duke Looks Like a Groomsman
- The Valet Who Loved Me
- Save a Horse, Ride a Viscount
- Earl Lessons

ABOUT THE AUTHOR

Valerie Bowman grew up in Illinois with six sisters (she's number seven) and a huge supply of historical romance novels.

After a cold and snowy stint earning a degree in English with a minor in history at Smith College, she moved to Florida the first chance she got.

Valerie now lives in Jacksonville with her family including her two rascally dogs. When she's not writing, she keeps busy reading, traveling, or vacillating between watching crazy reality TV and PBS.

Valerie loves to hear from readers. Find her on the web at www.ValerieBowmanBooks.com.

facebook.com/ValerieBowmanAuthor

twitter.com/ValerieGBowman

instagram.com/valeriegbowman

goodreads.com/Valerie_Bowman

pinterest.com/ValerieGBowman

bookbub.com/authors/valerie-bowman

amazon.com/author/valeriebowman

Made in United States
North Haven, CT
01 August 2022

22107979R00139